About the author

Y.B? is an anonymous author, originally from The Netherlands. The author spent several years travelling the world and working for non-profit organisations. The author started writing *The London Hero* whilst living in New Zealand, and finished the work in Belgium, where the author still resides.

THE LONDON HERO

Y.B?

THE LONDON HERO

Vanguard Press

VANGUARD PAPERBACK

© Copyright 2021
Y.B?

The right of Y.B? to be identified as author of
this work has been asserted by her in accordance with the
Copyright, Designs and Patents Act 1988.

All Rights Reserved

No reproduction, copy or transmission of this publication
may be made without written permission.
No paragraph of this publication may be reproduced,
copied or transmitted save with the written permission of the
publisher, or in accordance with the provisions
of the Copyright Act 1956 (as amended).

Any person who commits any unauthorised act in relation to
this publication may be liable to criminal
prosecution and civil claims for damages.

A CIP catalogue record for this title is
available from the British Library.

ISBN 978-1-80016-092-7

*Vanguard Press is an imprint of
Pegasus Elliot MacKenzie Publishers Ltd.*
www.pegasuspublishers.com

First Published in 2021

**Vanguard Press
Sheraton House Castle Park
Cambridge England**

Printed & Bound in Great Britain

Dedicated to change; I am coming for you

I truly hope one day my
mind will be cleansed and
freed in such a way, that I
no longer ache to be in
pain.

14-07

My walls aren't vertical, they're horizontal.
And I didn't build them for you,
I built them for me.

CHAPTER 1

There is not much to come back for,
but there is also no more reason to stay away.

'Is she going to make it?'

An eerie silence fell between them. The intensive care unit was oddly quiet. No one had said the words out loud, but everyone wished they had received more patients.

The doctor standing next to him scraped her throat and gave him the rundown of the situation.

'I can't give you any guarantees at this stage. If she pulls through the first twenty-four hours, I will be able to tell you more. The injuries she has sustained are… they're quite severe. And then, of course, there's the emotional component, which makes it even harder to judge the situation at this stage.'

Agent Curtis had his gaze fixed on the young woman. Today's events in London made him sick to his stomach. The nurses had positioned the young woman's body in a peaceful way, which made it look like she was sleeping and could wake up any time. It gave him a false sense of security, nothing about it was real. His brain registered what his eyes saw, but his soul refused to believe any of it.

'The biggest milestone would be for her to start breathing on her own again.'

The doctor, whose name badge read Tisley, quickly glanced at the coffee cup in his left hand and noticed a slight discoloration on his ring finger. Many hands, all with different stories to tell, had held that cup during the time she had worked at the London hospital's intensive care unit. It was the coffee patients' relatives would drink when they'd spend the night not wanting to leave their loved ones alone and praying everything would turn out okay. Sometimes it did turn out okay for those families, but sadly sometimes it did not.

The forty-some-year-old, took a small sip of his coffee, his gaze still fixed on the woman. His skin was pale, and his eyes looked as if he'd just been crying. There was nothing left in his eyes, no fire or anger. Just emptiness.

'Hang in there, Agent Curtis,' Dr Tisley told him, as she lightly laid her hand on his elbow. Then she turned around and walked away through the long white hallway, onto her next patient.

The buzzing from his phone startled him and he took his gaze off the young woman.

'Yes?'

He didn't like stretching phone conversations too much, not on the work floor at least. They were meant to be to the point and effective. His agents knew that about him, and within ten seconds he had hung up the phone again. He looked at the woman one last time, hoping she would still be alive when he'd return, but knowing he would be one of the very few to feel that way about her.

He turned around and left the young woman to fight on her own. On his way out, he abandoned the cup in a rubbish bin.

***

The hospital was busy. It surprised him. He had expected the hospital to have worked through its rush-time by now. He looked around the emergency room and wondered what all these people would do if they knew it was him. At some point, when the world did know it was him, they would have his face imprinted on their retinas. He'd be famous, admired and hated. He was excited for his future, but he was also relieved to keep a low profile for the time being.

He walked up to the reception desk, where a nurse was busy answering phone calls from distressed family members and media channels. The red lights on the sides of the device told him all lines were busy.

She looked at him briefly, but didn't utter a word in his direction. He realised he looked and acted too calm for this scenery, but he couldn't help himself. He thrived under these circumstances — the panic, the fear, the drama, the adrenaline. Those were the components he needed to create a calm atmosphere inside his mind. This was his Valhalla, and he wanted it to last as long as it possibly could.

Unfortunately, part of his job was blending in. And being the only calm person in the emergency room made him stand out like a sore thumb. He couldn't draw attention to himself, it would jeopardise the rest of his mission.

He took off his vest and was glad to see that the blood had turned most of the bandage dark red, leaving a red mark on his shirt. Just as he wanted to take a seat, a woman rushed to his side — his plan to attract attention had worked.

'Sir, what happened to you? Were you a victim of the bombing?' Her puffy, red eyes indicated she must have been working her second shift of the day. Her slim and fit body stood in front of him, dressed in dark blue scrubs. Her blonde hair, tied in a ponytail, had started to slip off the top of her head and was now hanging loosely on her neck. Clearly, she hadn't had a second of peace since the first injured person had been brought in.

'Yes, I am. I know you are busy, so I tried to fix it myself, but it just keeps bleeding.' He was a great actor and he knew it. He could create a sympathetic encounter in seconds.

'All right, I need you to come with me.'

She went ahead and pulled up a chair in a place where there had been a bed before. He sat down and looked around the room, created by green curtains.

'You're awfully calm,' she noticed.

'I'm used to it.'

She looked at him, clearly unsure what he meant by his remark. For a moment she seemed fearful.

'It happens a lot around here,' he quickly explained to her, using a Middle Eastern accent. 'How many?' he asked, and mimicked a concerned facial expression, but she didn't look at him.

She removed the bandage and disinfected his arm. 'I don't know. Hundreds are injured, I'm sure. I don't know how many have lost their lives, though.'

He detected a trace of a foreign accent; he just couldn't place it. 'Have you lost anyone today?' He didn't make eye contact, but instead stared at the floor, feeling scared a hint of pride might show on his face.

'I don't know yet.' Her eyes filled with tears as she pushed her teeth tightly together to stop herself from showing any more emotion.

She injected him with a local anaesthesia about an inch above the wound and wiped away the small dot of blood left behind by the needle. Blood was still pouring out of the wound and she handed him another bandage to stop the bleeding, as she injected a second local anaesthesia an inch below the wound. She put the needle down on the tray and looked him straight in the eye.

'I hope they stone the person responsible.'

He looked at her. The expression should have connected with him in some way. Anger, fear, anything. Instead, he smiled. There was something about her he liked; a certain fire, a certain boldness. To his surprise, she smiled back at him.

'The anaesthesia will take a few minutes to work. I'll be back with you shortly and stitch you up. Then you can go home.'

He nodded in response and watched her walk away.

***

Her eyes stared at her own reflection in silence. It wasn't often she felt this unsure about her next move. Either way, her action had consequences. There were two options to choose from, both with such different outcomes it made her uneasy. Yet for some reason she also knew it wouldn't matter, her future was written in the stars somehow. Regardless of what decision she made now, the outcome would remain the same. Because both had a common denominator: her. In either situation, she had the possibility to change her circumstances, and in that she could find true freedom. She could feel powerful.

However, at this given moment, she didn't feel powerful. She felt overwhelmed by a choice she couldn't make. It was as if her heart and her brain were both pulling her in opposite directions. She needed to feel in control again, that would make everything better. And so, staring at her own face, looking at all the imperfections, redness, small spots, hairs and blemishes, she tried to find ways to feel powerful in both hypotheticals.

Her body was in pain and she couldn't understand why. Her mind worked perfectly fine, noting and noticing everything going on around her. In fact, her mind hadn't been this sharp in a long time. It was as if she was on some drug which helped her focus. Street drugs were out of her comfort zone, though — pills and alcohol were her poison. But street drugs she had never touched, she had seen it go horribly wrong too many times in her line of work.

Although she didn't move, her muscles ached and she could feel her organs crying out for help. The body she had fought to destroy was shutting down and it felt so peaceful to finally not have to look after it any more.

Her mind was still here, working full speed, better than it ever had before. Her body was useless, she didn't need it any more. Right here, in this moment, she could stay forever. Looking at herself, staring into her soul and not having to worry about anyone interrupting the highly intellectual connection and conversations the people inside her head were having — it was peace.

Not once did she stop to consider telling herself it was okay to disappoint. Whichever way life would go, people would be disappointed in her. And whichever way life would go, she would try and please people, even if it meant she wouldn't be okay. Not once did she stop to consider telling herself it was okay to choose happiness, to choose mental health over missed opportunities.

All she noticed was having to close one door and the fear of the possibility that another might not open again. She needed a moment of insane courage to give her power so she could decide her life.

Deep down, she already knew what needed to be done. Heart versus brain, it didn't matter. The common denominator would eventually balance out life in the way it had always intended to run.

People live their lives by the grace of the encounter. Throughout her life she had painted a picture in her mind of who she wanted to be. At first, she was scared to admit it to herself, then to say it out loud, then to act on it, and finally, to admit it to others.

Her hazel brown eyes moved from her reflection to the inside of her left wrist. There was something there that shouldn't have been there. The fact that it was should have given her enough direction to decide on what needed to happen. There was also something missing, something she wanted to be there. *Let pleasure be your plan, you deserve it.*

Whichever way she twisted it, the outcome would be the same. It would mean *him*. She just needed to decide which road to take; the healthy one, or the addictive one.

At last, she looked back at her reflection and allowed herself to smile.

It took nearly forty-five minutes for her to return, during which time no one else had even looked at him. Far more seriously injured people had the right of way before him. When she returned, her face had gone pale. She closed the curtain.

He realised it wasn't so much for his privacy as it was for hers. She grabbed the necessary utensils, once again cleaned the wound and tested to see if the anaesthetic still had its full effect, which he comforted her in saying that it did.

Without saying a word, she pushed her fingers into the wound and took out a tiny piece of metal. She held it out in her hand and then put it in a plastic cup on the tray.

'That'll go to the lab,' she broke the silence within the curtains. 'Although I doubt it'll be of much use.'

In all his years of experience, he had never had a piece of his art removed from his own body. He wanted to ask her if he could keep it, as a trophy. But he knew that would put him to the top of the suspect list. Middle Eastern male, immigrant, who asks to take home a piece of the bomb as a keepsake. The thought made him smile, but he quickly changed his facial expression when she locked eyes with him.

'Strange to think that...' He didn't finish his sentence.

She nodded. 'We, ehm…' She pushed her teeth together again, shaping a hard jawline. 'We just lost a little boy because of that little piece of shitty scrap metal.'

Little piece of shitty scrap metal. How dare she insult his art. He wisely kept his mouth shut, although within his mind there were hundreds of different responses shaping themselves, each more aggressive than the previous one.

'I need you to relax your arm.'

He realised he had made two fists and quickly relaxed his posture, before giving her a faint smile.

'He was only ten… The look on his parents' face… I will never forget it.'

She had finished the first stitch. Again, she looked him straight in the eye, searching for any sign of comfort.

He said nothing, nor did he give her the calming smile that had worked for her before. A chill rolled down her spine, his cold eyes had rejected her. It was as if he hated her emotion.

She quickly got to work on the second stitch. She could just be imagining it. Perhaps he, too, had lost someone the same way, and all of this brought back memories.

'Forgive me. I shouldn't be discussing any of this with you. You are the patient and I am the nurse, not the other way round.' She smiled warmly at him, her way of asking for forgiveness.

He nodded shortly. *Little piece of shitty scrap metal. How dare she.* All empathy he had felt towards her had disappeared in a heartbeat. Although he did still feel attracted to her. There was something about the way she moved, the way she spoke.

He counted the stitches. Four down. Another five to go, he estimated.

She had finished the last stitch and placed the utensils on the tray next to him. The silence annoyed him. He knew there wasn't much time left for the two of them to spend together, if he didn't say something to comfort her now.

She was only young, and suddenly he realised perhaps she hadn't had the opportunity to fall in love with that scrappy metal the way he had. Judging by the cross around her neck she could have had a protective upbringing, close to God. Her mission may have been a different one, and besides, she also did not know he had been the creator of the art. There was always the possibility she was hiding amongst the humans, too, feeling a desire to act on behalf of God to bring goodness into the world the way he had done tonight. She could have faked empathy the same way he had plenty of times. But if she had, she was a great actress.

He looked at her face again and could not detect any emotion. As if it had disappeared from her face, only to return when human interaction required it to be there. He gently touched her arm.

'Forgive me, too. It's been a long night.'

She looked him in the eye. A sigh of relief came over her, and he noticed it. She wanted to be his friend. He wasn't wrong; there was an unmistakable connection between the two of them.

She smiled at him again, a real smile this time. 'Yeah, it really has.'

'What time do you get off?'

She shrugged. 'The hospital called everyone in. I think I won't get off until tomorrow morning.'

'It is tomorrow morning.' He showed her his watch. Half past one.

'Oh, well in that case I won't get off until some time around ten, I guess. I hope I'll be able to get some sleep between now and then.'

A part of him wished to take her out and whisk her away, but he knew he could not. She would jeopardise his mission.

CHAPTER 2

Jack Binckle parked his car at the personnel entrance of The Royal London Hospital's emergency room. As he tapped his fingers on the steering wheel, the forty-one-year-old reporter caught a glimpse of himself in the rear-view mirror. A scruffy, unshaven man stared back at him. It had been a year since he was laid off and it hadn't done much good for his mental health.

He opened the glove compartment and took out an orange bottle of pills. The anti-depressants had been the next step, alcohol had been the stepping stone. It had been a calculated move; one he knew would take him down a darker path. His general practitioner, a slim Chinese man in his thirties who he had seen twice in his life, had laid out the path towards obtaining the pills. There would need to be three consultations before he could prescribe them. It was a matter of precaution, he had explained, as the pills carried the risk of side effects, one of which being depression. The irony hadn't struck the young Chinese doctor.

Midway through his first consultation, Jack Binckle knew he wouldn't come back for the second and the third, but instead he had started his search for a different general practitioner, preferably one who was using the pills himself. He had found one, a middle-aged white male only a few years away from retiring. A capable, caring man, nonetheless, but no longer a stickler for the rules and someone who didn't believe the latest research. Within five minutes of meeting him, his new GP had scribbled down a prescription for Prozac in a handwriting only a pharmacist would be able to read.

The last pill found its way down his throat without a single sip of water as he observed the hospital's staff entrance. Two obese nurses walked towards the green doors, talking, laughing and showing no signs of sadness, despite the earlier events. He knew what he was doing was not going to make him very well-liked in London, but he needed a quick buck.

He quickly got out of his car and caught the door just before it slammed shut. The long white hallways had no effect on him. In his family there were no sad tales of cancer or heart disease. There was pain, but the pain he felt wasn't in his body, it was in his mind. And in his experience, no hospital could cure that kind of pain.

Quickly navigating through the hospital, he found his way onto the ICU, which was remarkably quiet and smelled like Dettol. A female doctor slid a door closed behind her and noted down her latest test results, before handing over the clipboard to one of the preoccupied nurses at the front desk.

Less than half of the available rooms had patients in them and Jack Binckle at once recognised the person he had come for. Besides the female doctor, there was only one nurse present in the ICU. Whoever ran the hospital had moved all available staff onto the emergency room, expecting a huge flood of people to come through the doors today.

One last glance at the hallway he had left behind him showed him no one was around, and he quickly disappeared into the young woman's room.

Utter shock replaced the adrenaline he had felt sneaking into the hospital. The sight of the young woman reminded him of the ugliness London had had to deal with. An unaccounted number of bodies lay in the rubble and the families of those victims would never be the same again. A sense of remorse came over him. Jack Binckle had done unethical things to showcase the truth behind a story; breaking and entering, stealing and the occasional threat were methods to get his job done. But he had never broken moral, for just a pay check. Desperate times called for desperate measures.

He walked closer to the young woman and tried to take in her features, which were hidden underneath dried blood from cuts she had sustained. Her pale face had a tube sticking out of it, her chest slowly moved up and down along with the pumping and beeping of the machinery next to her. She had scratches and bruises all over her arms and a big cut in her right ear. When he looked below her waist, he knew that if she ever were to regain consciousness, she would never fully recover.

Jack Binckle stepped back and did what he had come to do. He took a picture of her pale face and then her whole body. He lowered the camera and took one last look, when he realised she wore a hospital tag around her left wrist. For a moment he doubted whether he should, but then decided he would ultimately regret it if he didn't. He wouldn't necessarily need to give her name to any media station, he could hold on to it for a while until it suited him to use it.

Voices and footsteps came nearer the young woman's room. Quickly he lifted her left wrist, turned it over, laid it back down and took his picture. He slipped the camera into his bag and fled back into the hallway as he thought of what he had just seen.

***

Interpol Director Wayne Kneebone turned off the television hanging on the wall opposite his desk. His top-floor office offered a spectacular view of the city. London's Tower Bridge, The London Eye and Buckingham Palace all in one glance. But today that magnificent view showed nothing but hatred. He walked over to the window and looked down on the people he had vouched to protect.

'This is bad, Patrick. Soon the media will start broadcasting speculations, the public will follow. And before you know it, we are creating a situation that's even more dangerous than the one we are in now. We've got to give them something. Something to make them believe it's all not as bad as it looks.'

Patrick was sitting on one of the many desk chairs at the long chestnut conference table, his feet resting on its top.

'But how? We've got nothing. No suspects and no other leads.' Patrick looked at his boss, who had also become one of his closest friends over the past few years. His grey suit fitted him nicely and fell perfectly over his broad shoulders. His hair had started turning grey about a year earlier and now matched the colour of his suit. The stress had gotten to him, although he would never admit to that.

Sirens were flashing far beneath him. Small dots represented the police and masses of innocent bystanders who were all in some way involved in the horrific crime that had hit his city today. He dreaded the questions the reporters would ask him. It was the same story over and over again. The authorities should have been aware of the sleeper terrorist cell, but they weren't. Then he had to go ahead and come up with a reason why they weren't.

Truth was, because they simply hadn't had the time, money or manpower to go out and check every potential threat. Of course, he would never be able to say that out loud. It would make Interpol look weak, and then, in turn, it would make the United Kingdom look weak. No, he had to set up a strong front. Fight fire with fire.

He could not bear another press conference where reporters without any law enforcement experience would shout at him and tell him how to do his job. Reality was, every now and then these things would happen, under any leadership. It didn't make it any less wrong or any easier to deal with, but there would never be a government in which such things would stop happening.

Sometimes he wished he could bring up all the terrorist attacks they had prevented. But there was a rule against that, one he understood. If they were to pride themselves with all the prevented attacks, no one would ever feel safe again.

'If only people knew how many attacks we have prevented. Just in the past six months alone,' he eventually said.

'Yes. I agree. They'd be a little less hard on you. But it wouldn't change anything in the end.'

'I know, I know.'

The phone on his desk rang.

Patrick got up to answer as Kneebone stayed put, watching the flashing as he dreaded the final casualty count.

CHAPTER 3

My dearest stranger,

What if I told you I wanted to die? Would you forgive me? Would you try to understand and not blame me?

Because the truth is, I've always told myself that self-harm wasn't about wanting to die, but merely about punishing myself and feeling pain. Now, however, I am not so sure any more.

At times I want the darkness to take me away, because it'll be more peaceful for me. I know it would cause inconsolable heartache for you, which is why I continue to be strong and why I continue to fight. But sometimes, those days where I have to fight against this darkness, feels like inconsolable heartache, too.

I'm scared to tell you the truth, the whole truth and nothing but the truth. Scared to be judged and sentenced for it, afraid you will never consider me to be the strong, fun-loving woman again. Afraid you'll be afraid of leaving me on my own.

I don't want you to be upset or scared each time I'm having a tough day. I don't want you to have to wonder whether I'd hurt myself if you left me alone. And I also don't want to be looked upon as crazy, because I am not.

Crazy is a great term when referring to art or fun. It's the worst you could call me when referring to my mental health. I have overcome more than some will ever have to worry about, and I continue to win with each day I spend on this earth.

I can't deny the fact, however, I am always fantasising about leaving this earth. You are truly the only reason I am still here. If it wasn't for you, I would have left a long time ago.

It's strange, because guilt is keeping me from committing such an act, although I wouldn't have to deal with the guilt any more because I would be gone.

I'm causing you pain with the little bit of truth you know. It's the reason I don't tell you just how far gone I am and how much further gone I was.

I'll be honest and finally say the words out loud: I am an alcoholic, I am addicted to cutting, I suffer from episodes of severe depression and I starve myself purposely.

I know which events caused me to go down this path so far, all of which are too heart-breaking for me to tell you about.

Again, I fear your judgement, even though I am aware I should be facing these traumas rather than run from them. But I also know the episodes of depression started occurring much earlier in my life, I think around the age of six. So, a long time before any traumas.

I want you to know I fight every day to choose healthy tools to work on my healthy mindset.

Please forgive me for my depressive mood swings or distant behaviour. I am always aware I am not me, and it hurts me to see you wonder why. It's why I stay away and retreat.

It's not you, it's me.

Still yours,
with love from afar.

CHAPTER 4

I think people choose to believe in faith because they
are scared to act upon what they want.

There is a strict protocol in place for dealing with the aftermath of attacks like these. A protocol anyone in law enforcement ought to know by heart, regardless of their ranking or agency.

Using the little information the local police had received, they had arrived on the scene first and tried to create some order in the chaos. Evacuating the public had been their first step, before securing the perimeter by shutting down all entrances and exits with crime-scene tape. After that they had started taking statements from anyone who had seen something. Of course, by that time the people who had really seen something were either on their way to the hospital or they had fled the scene, in severe shock.

Early on into taking witness statements it had become painfully obvious there'd be no survivors on ground zero. The ones who had walked away from the explosion unharmed or mildly injured hadn't been anywhere near the bomb and quite simply didn't know anything. There were no descriptions of any person acting suspiciously. They asked as many witnesses as possible about their specific whereabouts when the bomb had gone off, and they had all answered various positions — hallways, public bathrooms, any platforms, and so on. All positions were mentioned, except one: platform six.

Interpol, having its headquarters only a few blocks away from the scene, had arrived barely fifteen minutes after the explosion. Agent Curtis and his team knew from experience not to put too much faith in witness statements after an attack like this. Most people spoke out of fear; each Arab was a bomber and each Caucasian person was a victim.

Frustrated with the lack of information, Agent Curtis had decided it was time to move to this crime scene's ground zero; platform six. They wouldn't be the first ones down there. Braver men and women had gone inside before them. EMT's and local police had run towards the place victims and survivors had been running away from. They had carried the seriously injured out of the building and had calmed the panicked ones.

And then some of those EMT's and local police had arrived on platform six, the place where it would never be the same. It was obvious at first glance, no one could have survived an attack like this. That is until they had heard a soft groan and had pulled a young woman from underneath the rubble.

***

It was clear where the bomb had been. The meters adjacent to the spot had turned into somewhat of a crater. The people who had been standing closest to it were unrecognizable. They weren't even people any more, just body parts — there would be a lot of closed caskets. The brown-yellow floor had turned a coal black, here and there coloured with red swipes and puddles of human blood.

And here Interpol's anti-terrorism squad stood silently amidst the rubble and bodies. Each member of the elite team had seen crime scenes like these, but they also wished each time it would be their last. This time felt different, this time it was closer to home. Not even closer, it was their backyard. Never mind the heinous aftermath of politics and protocols they would have to deal with, the possibility of finding someone they knew, someone they loved, among the bodies lying at their feet was very realistic.

But this moment was theirs. The only moment in time they could take to comprehend what had happened, to wish there had been a different outcome and to mourn the losses. Because as soon as they stepped outside of the Underground, they would be subjected to judgement. They would be required to be professional and forget about human emotion. They would be expected to perform as robots.

The air lingered of peace, the kind of peace one might experience looking out at sea or watching a colourful sunset. There was no suffering any more in that moment in-between. That space in time where the struggle is finally over and the fear has left. The moment before you start fearing the pain of mourning, the small place in time where you're glad it's over and you feel a sense of relief.

For the people waiting outside, still unaware and praying, hell had already arrived. Some people would be lucky, and they would be spared another moment in hell. Whereas others would experience hell on earth, forced to come to terms with what had happened.

No one should have been there that day, everything should have gone differently. The smallest change in a daily routine could have changed and diverged lives dramatically. If only a child would have realised they had forgotten a book at home, if only the pregnant lady had decided to use her bathroom one last time before heading out for work. Those minutes, those small decisions could have saved their lives and altered the lives of their loved ones dramatically.

Society wouldn't have allowed them to take those few extra minutes, scared they would be late for commitments. Now they would be late forever. Gone eternally. They were dead and there would be an uncontrollable range of emotions expressed by the ones left behind.

Outside, there were people who wanted to know exactly what it looked like down here, in the chill tunnel which had turned into a mass grave. Inside, no one wanted to know. Of course, the latter desire remained a secret. This was the job the squad had signed up for and regardless of the pains and sorrows, it was the job the nation expected them to do.

'All right guys, let's get to work,' Curtis spoke. 'Rowan, I want you to photograph each body. Edmonds, your attention should be on finding pieces of the bomb, and get everything labelled. Joan and Katrina, get the bodies organised as soon as they are photographed.'

'On it,' Rowan replied. His voice sounded harder than he had intended.

'Yeah… on it,' Edmonds forced herself to say.

She was glad to have Curtis to fall back on. For once she didn't feel the need to prove herself by taking charge. She hid her face behind a mouth mask and put on latex gloves. With each move she made, the white, plastic-like texture of her overalls, covering her body from head to toes, made a chafing noise. It was that noise and the sounds of cameras flashing which filled the emptiness of the Underground tunnel.

Edmonds glanced over to Rowan, who had just begun photographing one of the bodies. Each member of the team was busy collecting evidence and photographing every inch of the scene, but simultaneously, like an unspoken rule, everyone had steered away from the children's bodies. The way they were unrecognisable scared Edmonds the most. Again, the camera's flicker went off, permanently taking possession of a moment everyone would want to forget about.

She needed to let it go, only then would she be capable of doing her job and ensuring justice was done for the ones left behind. A quality which she had mastered over the past few years and also one which made men refer to her often as 'cold'.

Her legs felt as if they weighed a hundred tons as she walked towards the crater-like shape near the staircase. It was there she would find bigger pieces of the bomb, but it was also there where she would have to physically step over parts of what used to be people. It took great effort as she set her foot, covered in white plastic, over the remains of what looked like a leg.

Over on the other side towards the wall where the benches used to be, Rowan had just arrived at one of the children's bodies. He considered himself to be too much of a professional to show emotion on cases like this. Nevertheless, he too, had to close his eyes for a moment to escape the gruesome scene of which he was now a part.

It had been a small group of friends and, roughly estimated by the length of their mutilated bodies, they were between the ages of eight and twelve. His thoughts didn't sink any further than right there in that moment. He didn't think about their parents, instead, he hoped they hadn't felt any pain. He quickly and silently spoke a small prayer for them. Hoping it would help their souls, but mainly hoping it would give him some peace.

He opened his eyes again and continued as if nothing had happened, feeling Edmonds' eyes burning in his neck. There was only one superior, their team leader. But since he had more experience than her and had joined the team nearly a year before her, he felt somewhat obligated to take charge when Curtis wasn't around. And in this moment, he wanted to show her how to put emotion aside — the victims needed justice. Dealing with the aftermath of the horrific things they had seen would have to wait till later.

The most crucial part would come in now: determining whether the bomber had left behind a trace of himself. Whether it had been a suicide bomber or a command attacker.

Edmonds knew from experience that command attackers often used IED containers, such as a briefcase or backpack. Small objects like these were common and easy to place. You couldn't possibly suspect everyone with a briefcase or a backpack to be carrying a bomb. Although the survivors of this heinous attack would adopt that mindset for many weeks, months, if not years to come. The fear they'd feel each time they'd be in public was unimaginable for Edmonds.

From the moment she had walked into the Underground, she had felt something was off about the crime scene. The complete lack of witnesses had frustrated her, but also scared her. In the crater, there were only pieces of what used to be a briefcase. A suicide bomber would have tied the explosives to his body, often leaving his shoes standing where the bomber had stood. That wasn't the case here.

'Found something!' Her voice echoed throughout the tunnel and she immediately regretted shouting. It felt disrespectful.

Curtis walked over to the small object Edmonds held out for him and opened an evidence bag. The piece of shrapnel seemed so blameless in the big plastic bag. It was hard to believe that it was a piece of what had destroyed so many lives.

'Seems like it's a part of a cell phone, but the wire attached to it makes me think this was used as a detonator,' Edmonds thought out loud.

'I think you're right.' He took a closer look at the piece before continuing, 'Now that we know what to look for, I'm hoping we can find some sort of a signature. An attack like this takes planning and a sick mind. I'm sure the person placed a piece of his or her identity into making this bomb.'

'You think we might be able to trace it back to someone?'

'Perhaps.'

Edmonds followed Curtis' glance up and down the tunnel.

'What is it?'

'The nails in the bomb caused extra damage, part of the reason so many people died.' He paused, looking around. 'What time would the next train have arrived?'

'Ehm… 8.29 a.m., according to the sign I saw outside.'

'And yet, he detonates the bomb at 8.27 a.m.. Why wouldn't he wait another two minutes? He'd do more damage.'

Before Edmonds could agree with him, he had walked closer to the track.

'This is where the doors would be, it's where people would be waiting to get on and where everyone getting off would push themselves into the crowd.'

Again, he looked around, as if in haste. 'How many Underground doors do you think can open between the staircase and the actual tunnel?'

Edmonds looked from left to right, estimating the distance in her head and imagining the Underground train pulling up. 'I'd say at least five or six.'

'Five or six places where he could have pretended to bump into someone, drop his briefcase, get on the Underground, make his call from a safe distance and detonate the bomb. Instead—' Curtis walked alongside the track towards the staircase, knowing he was onto something '—he placed the bomb here, against the staircase.'

A feeling of unease came over him.

'We found our only survivor on that side of the staircase, in the only spot where the nails couldn't get to her. Everyone else died because of the impact of the explosion or the nails in them.'

'So...' Edmonds tried following his train of thought. 'She's either very lucky, or she's in on it in some way?'

'She's not in on it.'

Curtis' voice travelled and made Rowan look up from one of the bodies. He wanted to join in on the brainstorming session, but simultaneously felt as if he'd be interrupting something.

'How do you know for sure? You always say...'

'I know what I always say,' he interrupted her, something he never did. 'But this time is different. She's not in on it.'

But how do you... Edmonds wondered. She was never afraid to speak her mind, not even to her superiors, but she knew it was a moment where she'd better stop talking. Even if she had been able to finish her question, Curtis would not have heard it; he had already walked up the stairs and away from the crime scene.

***

'At 8.27 a.m. this morning a bomb went off in London's Underground at Westminster station. None of the authorities here today have confirmed the number of casualties, but since we've been here only unharmed or mildly injured people have left the Underground. As you can see behind me, it's hard to imagine rescue workers

will be finding any survivors who were on the platform on which the bomb detonated, which is said to be platform six.

'This is the third attack London has suffered in the past year and by far the worst we've seen in many years. Sources have not confirmed, but speculations are that this is, in fact, a terrorist attack. As we speak, local authorities are evacuating all other public transport platforms around London and are advising everyone to stay away from public places.

'Judging by the agents who are currently on scene, it's Interpol who will be leading this investigation. They are on site processing the scene and aiding rescue workers.

'As you can see behind me, it's a coming and going of local police, EMT's and special agents all trying to determine the damage and searching for clues in relation to the person or group responsible for this heinous crime. Special Agent Francis Curtis oversees the anti-terrorism unit within Interpol and will be the lead on this investigation.

'The UK's threat level has been raised to level four, meaning an attack is imminent.

'Interpol's press handlers, as of yet, haven't released a single statement to the public or the media explaining what has happened here or how many people have lost their lives today.

'The fact they haven't released a statement tells us they simply don't have a grasp on the situation. Over

the course of the past days the threat level was a 1, stating the UK as being safe. It seems to us Interpol, or any other agency for that matter, had no idea this act of terrorism was coming our way.'

Hearing the media disrespect Curtis like that, broke Flynn's heart. Knowing exactly which emotions were running through his veins, made him wish he could be there. Momentarily, he pondered going down there himself, but he decided it was a selfish move, wanting to be right next to him, in a moment of crisis like this one.

Interpol's IT specialist knew exactly what Curtis needed from him and blamed himself for feeling so weak and vulnerable. At this stage, all he could do for Curtis was to offer as much assistance in his field of expertise as possible.

He muted the television screen hanging above his computer screens and stared back at the failing video footage which he had received. It would take time to restore any of it, and then it would still remain doubtful whether any of it would be usable as evidence. The small chance of being able to use the footage to identify the person responsible was barely enough to make Flynn bother at all. He stared at his screen and couldn't help but look away from it, back to the television screen.

The blonde, female reporter kept on telling the same story and facts using different wording. Then, when she had run out of facts to discuss, she moved onto subjective reporting on the lack of response Interpol had given on the matter.

Everyone wanted to know how many casualties there were, who was responsible, and mostly, how it could have happened. Only weeks ago, parliament had approved a new, broader budget to support the anti-terrorism division. Not only within Interpol, but within many agencies around the country. People would undoubtedly start asking questions about their tax money.

The media station kept on showing the same footage; Curtis walking past the media personas on his way into the Underground, his team following closely behind him. Not one of them had responded to the cameras and reporters. So now, they were to blame for the lack of communication. Rather than keeping a respectful distance and allowing the team to do their job, the media stations had already condemned Interpol and their anti-terrorism unit as 'uncooperative'. Speculation on terrorism would soon take over the conversation, if it hadn't already.

In a moment of anger, Flynn reached for the phone, knowing very well he wasn't helping Curtis, but needing to hear his voice and hoping Curtis would feel the same way. The phone only rang twice before Curtis picked up, immediately asking Flynn to wait before speaking as he sought a quieter place to talk.

'How are you holding up?' Flynn asked, feeling relieved Curtis took the time to talk with him.

'Same as you, I suppose.'

The men paused. There were no words to describe such an act of terror.

'It's a mess,' Curtis said eventually.

'Yeah… I didn't know whether to call you. You had already left before I could… I just needed to know you're okay. We're going to get this done together, Francis.'

'We better. These people deserve justice. And… you can always call me. I just, I've got to go now. We're piecing together the bomb.'

'Yes, of course. As soon as I've got something, I'll let you know.'

'Great. Thanks.'

Curtis had hung up without saying anything further, leaving Flynn grateful for having had the minute and a half of conversation.

It instantly gave him the energy to continue with his work. Curtis had that effect on him, although he wished at times he wasn't so dependable on his attention or presence. But in moments like these there was space and acceptance for emotions like the ones he felt.

He turned off the television and focussed on the task at hand, hoping he would soon have an excuse to call Curtis again.

CHAPTER 5

There will never be someone who I will allow to truly get to know me.

'What went through your mind?'

Vanima sat across from her and fumbled with the textile of her shirt. She took herself back to the moment, as if in slow-motion.

'At first, nothing.' She spoke slowly, choosing her words carefully. It was the first time she had tried remembering the event willingly.

'I was completely taken by surprise… My mind was empty for a few seconds.' She looked up and added, 'Which doesn't happen a lot.'

A faint smile.

'Would you say you have a very active mind?'

Vanima nodded.

'There's never a moment where I am not thinking anything. There's always something happening in my mind. People are talking to me, inventing things or overthinking. Thinking ahead, thinking of the past. But mainly just fantasy. Crazy stuff.'

'You mean to say there's people telling you to do things?'

'God, no. I'm not that kind of crazy.'

Vanima pulled herself up, using the couch's armrest she was sitting on. Her leg had started to fall asleep, although that was impossible. Slowly, she started moving around the room. Short distances between the couch, a table, a chair and the window sill were doable without the use of crutches.

A proud feeling came over her. She felt good, confident. Not scared of the brain-lady. Vanima didn't need a therapist — she needed a gun and a badge.

'I prefer not to use the term "'crazy"'.'

Vanima rolled her eyes out of sight. *Whatever.*

'What is the point of us having this conversation?'

'You mean they did not tell you?'

She shook her head. The tingling sensation in her absent foot was starting to fade away and she sat down again in front of the brain-lady.

'You're here to be evaluated. To see if your mental health is up to par so you could potentially be carrying a gun.'

Vanima chuckled and shook her head. An arrogant move, she knew, but she didn't care.

'Let me tell you something. You're holding up this investigation. If I'm to be on this team, I'm going to need to be able to protect myself. I need a gun.'

'If you want a gun to protect yourself, I'm going to need you to and answer my questions first. Nobody should be able to access a gun without the right state of mental health,' she spoke firmly.

'You're against guns,' Vanima stated rather than asked.

'Guns are appropriate in some situations, but they should not be used by someone with mental health issues. That is where I stand, and that is why they asked me to evaluate you.'

Vanima realised she had no choice and gestured for the brain-lady to ask another question.

'Tell me what went through your mind when it happened?'

Vanima closed her eyes. Recalling it was easy, but thinking back slowly and undergoing the whole thing again was horrible.

'I told you. Nothing.'

'Yes, at first. But then? After the initial shock faded?'

Vanima looked at the tips of her boots. If you looked at her feet from this angle, you couldn't tell a difference. It was only when you went above the boot that the difference in her legs became obvious.

She spoke quietly, 'I knew I was going to die. Perhaps not physically, but I knew mentally I'd be dead for a long time.'

CHAPTER 6

You disappointed me today; touched me, when you should have listened. If you keep on touching my body, without touching my mind, I won't be able to trust you. Each time you touch my body, you neglect a piece of my soul.

The door hit the wall as he threw it open.

'I've got interesting news,' Curtis said, as he entered Kneebone's office.

Kneebone remained silent for a moment, in shock at his agent's disregard for basic ethics. Patrick, seated opposite his boss at the impressive Chesterfield desk, was quicker to respond. He rose to his feet and immediately attempted to remove Curtis from the office as he ordered him to wait outside.

'I think it's in all of our best interests if *you* go outside,' Curtis spoke to Patrick, keeping his eyes on Kneebone.

With a quick nod, Kneebone dismissed Patrick, who unwillingly and clearly insulted left the room.

'Agent Curtis, I hadn't expected you in my office until later for the official briefing. But since you're here now, I suppose this 'interesting news' couldn't wait?'

'I'm here because we have a survivor.'

Curtis' face expressed signs of anger.

'Agent Curtis. I understand these are extraordinary circumstances to be in and I know this attack hurts all of us personally, but those are no grounds for you to...'

'The survivor is Special Agent Alexandra Vanima,' Curtis interrupted him.

He watched Kneebone intently; it was only for a brief moment, but he could have sworn his director's face turned pale for a moment there. Keeping his hands in his pockets, he stood silently and waited for Kneebone to utter his first words of disbelief.

'Are you sure?'

'I am. Hundred percent certainty. I went to see her myself.'

'And did you...?'

'She's a Jane Doe in the hospital's records. Nobody knows who she is; no reporters have picked up on the news and the treating doctors are unaware of her status.'

'Good. Good. That's good.'

Kneebone paced back and forth behind his desk as Curtis indulged himself in the sight and decided to add to the stress his director was feeling.

'I told you one day this would all come back to bite you. And here's that day.'

To Curtis' surprise, his director remained silent after his sneer. Doubting whether Kneebone had heard him, he continued. 'Wayne, she is not just a survivor who happened to be at the wrong place at the wrong time. She is the *only* survivor. She might very well be the only person who can help us with this investigation.'

The latter argument was clearly meant to make Kneebone say something, but he didn't. He stood still and watched the wall before continuing to pace back and forth behind his desk.

Curtis realised his director might take a while shaping an appropriate response, and so he decided to take a seat in Patrick's chair. He unbuttoned his blazer, crossed his legs and folded his hands on his lap as he eyed his stressed director.

He had expected outrage, a game-plan, disgusting ethics. Instead, he had gotten silence. On some level it scared him to see his director so lost. In his entire career he had always known Kneebone to be a man of quick responses, but apparently tackling Special Agent Alexandra Vanima for a second time was too much for him to handle.

Taking advantage of his lost director, he decided to request something he had longed to see for quite some time. 'I'm going to need access to the sealed records. We have to cross-reference her past with anyone involved in this attack.'

Kneebone pondered the thought momentarily, but then took a seat and wrote down a password on a yellow piece of paper.

'This is for you and Flynn *only*. No one else is to see those files unless I give the authorisation. Understood?'

'Understood,' Curtis gave a small nod. He hadn't expected to be granted the password to his former colleague's files and he quickly shoved the paper into his pocket.

'Thank you, Agent Curtis. You are dismissed.'

Curtis looked at his director and stuttered, 'Uh-uh, b-but we need some sort of a plan regarding…'

'Thank you, Agent Curtis. That will be all for now.' Kneebone spoke with more authority, having recovered from the initial shock.

Curtis gave a quick nod again and walked out of the room. Once outside and away from Patrick's gazing eyes, he took out his cell phone and took a picture of the paper. Then he pressed the elevator button and decided to finally see what was in those files.

Curtis exited the elevator and walked onto the field agents' floor, which was chaos all-round. The tip line had been ringing consistently for the past four hours, but no one had given any valid information. If anything, the citizens of London were slowing down the process of trying to find out who had committed the unspeakable crime.

The office, which was usually well-organised, hosted agents from different agencies. Papers, laptops, iPads, iPhones and other high-tech equipment covered the desks and chairs in the communal area. Secretaries walked around the office, pouring coffee, refilling the water jugs or carrying folders marked 'classified'.

Everyone was on their phone, each one shouting louder than the other, trying to get their message across.

The sight alone gave him a headache. Each agent worked hard, but it seemed to be an 'every-man-for-himself'-type of situation rather than a team effort. The lack of leadership in this moment of crisis surprised him. The agency clearly needed guidance from their director, but Curtis knew he was lost himself.

Ignoring the chaos as much as he could, he quickly reached the other side of the communal area and walked to the office at the end of the hallway.

'What have we got so far?' he asked as soon as he closed the door behind him.

There was a sense of serenity in the office he had just entered. A peaceful environment in which he knew the IT specialist performed his best work, mainly because he did not allow anyone else to use his office, let alone his computers.

Six computer screens filled the tiny, dark room and showed six different things, all having to do with the bombing. Empty coffee cups and water bottles filled his desk, along with papers and cords. The only thing of emotional value was a picture of the two of them together. Curtis looked at it briefly and a sense of melancholy came over him.

Flynn spun his chair around and at once began his briefing. 'We've got footage of a middle eastern male entering the Underground. Wearing a black jacket, black jeans and black sneakers. He hides his face under a black ball cap and black-shaded sunglasses. Seems to know where the cameras are, because we do not have a single shot of his face.'

The footage playing on the screen nearest to the photograph, told the exact same story Flynn just had. The video played in a loop of five seconds, each time showing the same unknown man walking amidst the crowd of people who had become his victims.

'Don't we have more footage of this man?'

'Forensics sent over cameras from the platform. I am trying to reconstruct as much as I can from those tapes. But don't get your hopes up, they might be too damaged for me to reconstruct any of it.'

Flynn knew he had to be to the point. There was no time to spend on unimportant details, although it was acts like these that made him realise they should grab each moment and simply enjoy life. He saw this type of tragedy in his work often, but it had gotten harder for him to deal with over the last couple of months. They were always one step behind tragedy and could never take credit for prevented attacks. It hadn't bothered him at the beginning of his career, but lately he had started shifting his opinion. Mainly because the media always portrayed the agency as a failure.

Nevertheless, he had continued his work, not necessarily for himself, but for Curtis. Knowing he did something of value for the people within the agency got him through every rough patch in his daily job.

'What about footage from before he arrived at the Underground?'

'That's the part where it gets interesting. He arrived in an Uber.'

'In an Uber?' Curtis looked at Flynn in disbelief.

'I called the Uber company and tracked down the car, using its GPS and licence plate number. We found the car in the south of London about three kilometres from the crime scene, parked under a bridge. Agents discovered the driver, Kamal Abadi, in the boot. Someone shot him with a .38'

'Fuck!' Curtis rubbed his face with his hands.

Flynn, wanting to be as helpful as he could be, pulled up the driver's licence of Kamal.

'The Abadi family came to the UK as refugees about four years ago. Kamal and his wife, Zahidah, brought along their two daughters, both of which are in primary school. I already informed your team. They're heading to the Abadi residence now.'

Curtis stared at the photo on the screen. Brown, empty, hardened eyes stared back at him. It was hard to imagine a father of two could be capable of such a heinous crime.

'I've started digging into Abadi's bank statements. At a first glance, everything seemed all right. There's no job listed for his wife, and Kamal's only income appears to have been the one from driving an Uber. But then I did some further research and found out Kamal Abadi's got two bank accounts. One with the Picto Bank and one with the Bank of Kingdom. The one with the Bank of Kingdom is a shared account he holds with his wife. Nothing special there, just the regular income and outgoings like rent, electricity and groceries.

The second bank account, however, shows strange activity. He had an appointment at the Picto Bank on 3rd of January this year and made his wife an authorised person on the account. I called the bank manager with whom Kamal had the appointment and she told me Kamal's wife was not present at the meeting. She also told me he acted very anxious and that he had asked her whether his wife would be able to access the account in case he passed. 'You never know when something bad happens to you now, do you?' he had told her. She thought it was strange, but not strange enough to mention it to anyone.'

'Has there been any activity in his account?' Curtis interrupted.

'I was just getting to that,' Flynn continued. 'I just found out about this moments ago, but he made absolutely no deposits into this account during the meeting with the bank manager, but this morning his wife Zahidah showed up at the same branch where he opened his account, wanting to collect a huge pay-out from that account.'

'Okay, put Zahidah's picture out. I want every agent and officer in Europe to know what she looks like. Say she is part of the network who orchestrated this morning's bombing, she's possibly armed, and highly dangerous. Anyone who tries to go near her, must do so with extreme caution.'

'It'll be on everyone's screen within fifteen minutes. The thing is, Rowan and Edmonds are aware Kamal is dead, but are considering Zahidah to be a witness, not a suspect.'

'Don't inform Rowan and Edmonds about this just yet. I do not want them to create any suspicion towards Zahidah.'

'I will send you the address, assuming you will be heading over there immediately?' Flynn asked, hoping Curtis would stick around a little longer.

'I will shortly, but first I need you to get everything you can on Alexandra Vanima.'

'Alexandra Vanima? Her name sounds awfully familiar.' He was confused.

'She's our only survivor. And… she used to work for Interpol.'

'Ah, that Alexandra Vanima.'

A combination of excitement and astonishment urged Flynn to look away from Curtis' eyes and focus back on his screens. His fingers flew over the keyboard as he accessed the Interpol database and typed in Alexandra Vanima's name.

'The classified files. This is the authorisation code.' Curtis handed him the piece of paper.

Flynn accepted and smiled at Curtis. He felt his heart beating fast as Curtis came nearer to him and placed his hand on the back of his chair. He'd often do that. One hand behind his back, leaning on his chair, and one hand leaning beside him on the desk. He'd lean in close to have a good look at the things Flynn would show him on one of his screens.

'Right here…' He opened a file marked classified.

The men both started reading it with great interest. Everything she had told him was exactly right, and more.

'Oh my God, Francis.'

Curtis, still reading, put a hand on Flynn's shoulder and murmured, 'I know, I know.'

Knowing Curtis was a man of paper and pen, not screens and keyboards, Flynn started printing the necessary files.

'Have you told Kneebone yet?' Flynn asked, as if he had an epiphany.

'Yes. Who do you think gave the authorisation?' Curtis took his eyes away from the file and smiled broadly.

The smile made Flynn's heart beat fast again, and he wondered if Curtis experienced the same feeling. He chuckled, anticipating the answer to his next question. 'What did he say?'

Curtis laughed.

It was a long time since Flynn had seen him laugh. He seemed so relaxed in that moment. If only they could just stay there and live in that moment. If only Francis didn't have to walk out of his office and deal with hell.

If only they could just be in the moment and be happy. Be free, be at ease.

'He had no idea what to say. It took him a good minute before he had recovered himself. And when he finally did, the only thing he could manage to do was grant us access to the files before dismissing me.'

Flynn laughed. 'I wish I could have seen his face.'

'It was a terrific sight.'

Their eyes lingered a little longer, both wanting to enjoy the moment as long as they could.

Curtis scraped his throat and stepped back, which made Flynn get up and take the stack of papers out of the printer. He placed them into a paper folder and handed it to Curtis. For a brief moment their fingers touched, followed by a glance into each other's eyes that said more than an 'I love you' ever would.

CHAPTER 7

Hello again stranger,

That inner darkness returned to me today, without me asking. Everything was fine throughout the morning. The usual ups and downs followed me throughout the working day, but I just knew it was coming for me. I could sense it.

Nothing was out of place and it scared me, it made me incredibly nervous. There's something coming for me, I don't know what it is just yet. But I know, sooner or later, it'll come to turn my life upside down.

It's the unknown that scares me. I wish whatever it was could just come into my life now. The suspense is killing me. I've got no signs, no writing on the wall. But I know it's hiding for me somewhere.

Perhaps it's because everything is okay now. Work really was okay today. We got a lot of stuff done and managed to make a difference in people's lives.

But there is something inside me that tells me to be aware of everyone around me. No one can be trusted. There's something going on. I can see the way they look at each other when I enter the room. I think they know. I feel their eyes burning in the back of my head when I walk out of the room.

They were almost gone, and I didn't like that one bit. It worried me to have a wrist without visible battle wounds. Now they're back I feel more like me again. Without those battle wounds, who am I?

I wish I didn't have to hide it. That's what it all comes down to. It would change everything. Not hiding what I love, who I love, would make me, me.

I'd be proud of it in public, the way I am of it in private. I love what those scars stand for. I don't want them gone, just don't want to hide them.

But if I want to be able to continue to make them, I'm going to need to continue to hide it. My sober house isn't so sober any more.

Those moments of intense sadness. I wonder if they will ever go away. It's like I can't breathe when that happens. As if a thousand pounds weighs down on my chest.

Can't talk with it, can't walk with it. In those moments the only relief I can find is to cut a little piece of my flesh open, as if to release the darkness through that hole in my skin. I wish I didn't have to do that. Want to be done with it, but it keeps on finding its way back into the happy me. Like it chases me, hunts me down. Like how a cold heart chases the heat.

A battle of life and death. A race to the finish line will decide who wins. Either it'll kill me, and I'll live on forever, or I'll beat it and I'll be ordinary.

One thing is for sure, my secret must remain just that. I will kill before someone finds out.

Please continue to believe in me, stranger,
with love from afar.

CHAPTER 8

Close your heart, but keep me trapped inside.
Close your eyes, but always envision me.
Close your mind, but keep your dreams of me alive.

She placed two fingers in his neck and searched for his heartbeat.

'What are you doing?' He looked confused, but not enough to push her hand away. He liked her touch.

'Just testing a theory,' she said, with a dangerous, yet adorable smile.

His face turned red; his heart was racing. Her presence made him incapable of functioning. She knew now. She knew he was in love with her.

Her smile got broader and she moved her fingers away from his neck. Her eyes dazzled — he liked her. She had known it for some time, but to have it confirmed by a heartbeat and the colour of his face made her feel as if she could fly.

'Theory confirmed.' Another broad smile.

He chuckled and looked away. He wanted to pull her closer to him and enjoy her body heat. He wanted to kiss her on her forehead and hold her in his arms forever, but he was shy. Although he felt scared, she would not return his feelings, he could not handle not knowing for another second.

'Are you happy with the test results?' He smiled shyly, his face turning red again, and he quickly looked away.

He threw her off-guard. She thought she would have been in control of this little engagement, but he was smart and made a great comeback. She blushed and looked away. His beautiful eyes, like an ocean of love, portrayed a brightness in which she could drown. She chuckled; the word was out.

'Yes.' She looked at him, again drowning in his eyes.

He put his arm around her and pulled her body towards his. He placed a quick kiss on her forehead, she rested her head on his shoulder. Together they sat in silence on the bonnet of her car, admiring the lights of the city in which only days earlier a catastrophe had occurred.

It was hard to imagine a catastrophe like that had created such bliss for the both of them. The sun had set a long time ago, and a night breeze made her feel chilly.

Right there in that moment, that was true happiness. His warm embrace, the smell of her shampoo. They had only known each other for a short period of time, but this was true love.

***

Unspoken words flooded the air around them. Both were painfully aware this feeling couldn't possibly last, as is often the case with true love.

He thought back to the saying his parents had repeated many times: *all good things must come to an end at some point*. And this wasn't just good, this was amazing. This was the first time he had had the courage to undertake such an action. True things usually never started for him, because it required too many investments; one of which was the courage to get broken.

She took a deep breath, inhaling peace. There wouldn't be enough time to experience all the layers of their love, and it had already started to sadden her. She pondered the thought of kissing him, realising the moment had passed.

Perhaps they should have kissed, but there was no need to do so. A connection from soul to soul required each other's presence more so than each other's touch. Their souls were connected. A feeling you could get high on and stay high on for days.

High highs, incredibly low lows. Coming down from that drug, that was the moment she feared most. That's when that darkness would creep in. That's when she'd become needy and desperate for attention. Desperate to fight loneliness.

The problem was, loneliness couldn't be fought with other people's presence. It came from within and had to be fought from within. *I'm lonelier in crowds than I am when I am alone.*

And so, they sat in complete happiness, staring into the night, aware of each other's feelings and hoped for more time.

CHAPTER 9

Please don't allow me to run away.
I am scared to say: I really wish to stay.

'What do you want from us? Where is my husband?'

Zahidah tried fighting Rowan, but he sat her back down on the couch forcefully. Her younger daughter cried uncontrollably as the older tried comforting her little sister.

Rowan and Edmonds stuck out like a sore thumb dressed in their jeans, boots and dark coats, standing in the Middle Eastern, soberly decorated house. It was obvious the family did not have much money, but made ends meet.

'Ma'am. I need you to remain calm for a moment. Is there someone who can come and look after your daughters?' Edmonds asked.

The two girls were clearly too young to understand the severity of the situation. Zahidah ordered something in her mother tongue to her older daughter and the girls both disappeared up the stairs, out of the highly stressful situation.

'Ma'am. Do you know anything about this morning's bombing?'

The woman's soft crying irritated Rowan. 'Ma'am, I need you to stop crying and focus on what we're asking you.'

'I won't say a word until I know where my husband is.' Zahidah's defiance showed in her tone of voice, but her body language lacked every bit of it.

'Listen, Zahidah,' Edmonds started, 'I understand this is an extraordinary position for you to be in, but your husband dropped off the terrorist who detonated the bomb at the Underground. We just need to run over every tiny detail to make sure we can clear his name.'

Zahidah was fidgeting with a tissue she pulled apart in her hands. Her tears had turned into anger. These people had just come into her house and accused her husband of being involved in a terrorist attack on the city they both loved. The city that had given them a new, safe home.

'Please, Zahidah, just tell us anything you know so we can protect you and your family. Was Kamal acting more strangely lately? Did he leave the house at strange hours? Did you see him with anyone you don't know?'

Zahidah gave her an ice-cold look. Slowly and articulately, she repeated her demand. 'I will not speak with you until I see my husband.'

Fed up with Edmonds' empathic approach, Rowan decided to take the conversation a different way.

'Your husband is dead. Someone shot him in the head with a .38. We found him stuffed in the boot of his Uber. And now I am going to need you to tell me everything you know, or we'll put his damn picture on the six o'clock news saying he is our number one suspect.'

Zahidah got up from the couch and walked towards the window.

'You are lying. He can't be dead.' She turned around and looked at Edmonds.

Upon eye contact, the blonde woman looked to the floor in embarrassment. Zahidah shouted in her mother tongue and picked up a vase. Before she knew it, Rowan forced her down to the ground.

'Put your hands behind your back! Are you fucking crazy?' he shouted, as he struggled to keep the woman on the floor. Zahidah didn't give in and Rowan lashed out, leaving an ugly cut on her lip.

'Rowan!' Edmonds exclaimed, horrified.

He looked up and saw Zahidah's daughters in the doorway.

'Zara! Take your sister upstairs!' Zahidah's mother instinct took over and she stopped fighting.

Edmonds closed the door and helped Rowan place Zahidah on the couch. She sat down on the coffee table across from her and watched as the Syrian woman tried to stop her lip from bleeding.

'Ma'am. What do you know?'

'I don't know anything,' Zahidah answered submissively. 'Kamal… lately he was so stressed.'

Now that the emotions had got the better of her, she spoke with a heavier Middle Eastern accent.

'About a week ago, the doorbell rang at three a.m. When he went downstairs, I heard shouting. I tried looking out the window, but it was too dark to see anything. When he came back to the bedroom, he kissed me and said he needed to do a small job for a friend. He'd be back in one hour. Only he didn't come back until dinner time that day, and when he did, he looked as if he had seen a ghost.'

'Did he mention where he had been?'

Zahidah shook her head, blood still pouring from her lip.

'Did he say who had taken him or what they had talked about?'

'No. I tried asking, but he said nothing. I knew it was something bad.'

'What makes you say that?' Rowan intervened.

'Because I heard one of the men shout, 'You owe us, Kamal, so now it's time you give something back.'

'What language were they speaking?' Edmonds regained the lead of the conversation.

'Arabic.'

'Okay… Do you know if he took his car?'

'No, he did not. I remembered seeing it outside when I walked my girls to school.'

There was loud, impatient knocking on the front door and Rowan responded to it by getting up, purposely leaving the two women behind in the hopes Zahidah would open up more with him out of the way.

'Must be Curtis.'

As he walked out of the living room, he overheard Edmonds telling Zahidah to go clean her face in the kitchen as she'd check on her daughters. Edmonds was a good agent, he knew it. But their approaches were completely contradictory. Where he was direct, he found Edmonds too empathic for his taste.

'Rowan. How are we doing here?'

'Edmonds is talking to his wife. I think it's better if we give the two of them some space. Edmonds seems to have a connection with the wife.'

Curtis nodded. The two men didn't move from the hallway and kept the door to the living room closed.

'How are you holding up?'

'Doing okay. Just that sight of those kids, still in their school uniforms… I don't think I'll ever forget it.'

Curtis nodded again.

'You never will. But if you ever feel the need to talk about it… I hope you know I am 'here for you.'

'As am I for you.'

There was a brief, awkward silence between the men. The necessity to speak words, any words, eventually made Rowan shift the conversation.

'How is our survivor?'

'In a coma.' Curtis' voice hardened. 'Doctors aren't sure yet if she'll make it.'

Rowan's eyes searched the ground, not looking for anything. He knew this was not an easy time for his boss. Momentarily, he questioned whether to bring up his concerns regarding Curtis' well-being. But before he could, Curtis repeated his initial question.

Quickly, Rowan brought him up to speed, happy to regain his professional approach. 'Did Flynn find anything?' he ended his summary of events.

'Strange activity in Kamal Abadi's second bank account, and Zahidah knew all about it.' Curtis had quickly restored himself to the professional everyone knew he was and brought his team member up to speed.

A loud bang, sounding like a door slamming, alarmed both men. Immediately, they knew what had happened and ran into the kitchen, where they were just in time to catch a glimpse of the woman climbing the fence. Rowan tried to open the kitchen door as Curtis called for back-up. Only then did Rowan realise Zahidah had locked the door from the outside and the keys were on the floor.

'Fuck!' He banged the door powerfully, in an attempt to open it.

'What happened?' Edmonds had come down the stairs with Zahidah's two daughters.

'She's running! Let's go!' Curtis shouted. 'Edmonds, you stay here with those kids! Rowan and I will pursue.'

Before Edmonds could reply, both men had run out the front door, leaving her standing in the middle of the living room with two kids staring up at her, hoping she'd explain the situation. The younger one started crying again and she pressed both of them against her.

'Everything is going to be okay. Don't you worry,' she spoke softly, knowing it was unlikely they would ever see their mother again.

CHAPTER 10

Jack Binckle sat in his car and pondered his next move. The photo of the, so it appeared, sole survivor would sell for big bucks. It was the only tiny piece of hope the people of the United Kingdom could hold on to. And besides that, if she were to recover from her injuries, she'd potentially be the only witness to the heinous crime. Many friends and family of the victims would have questions for her. For a moment he smiled, he had just found the best source, and no other media station knew.

He got out of his car and walked into one of the local deli's. There was no one inside, except for the staff, who were all glued to the television screen. Jack Binckle scraped his throat, informing the staff they had a customer. Nobody moved, only the manager eventually walking over when he pointed at a ham and cheese sandwich sitting behind the counter. Without any verbal conversation, Jack Binckle laid the money on the counter as the manager handed him the sandwich and thanked him with a smile. Before he had walked out, the manager had already regained focus on the news.

He walked out of the deli and got back into his car, sunken deep into his own thoughts. He was about to take a bite of his sandwich when he heard a call for back-up on his police scanner. All units not on the bombing site were asked to respond immediately and go to an address on Townmead Road, not five minutes away from where Jack Binckle had parked his car.

Although owning a police scanner in the UK was illegal, he used it daily in his work as a freelance reporter. Ever since he had lost his job, he'd drive around the city, and sometimes even the country, to get a piece of a story or to get a shot he could sell to other media agencies. Wherever he went, his camera, tape recorder, an old brown notebook and a couple of pens were always in his bag.

At his former job he had been an outcast, too; always working odd hours and disobeying protocol laid on him by his superiors. It had been just that kind of behaviour which had gotten him fired. Protocol had forced him to undergo an exit interview in case he wanted to collect unemployment. He had smiled, even laughed, throughout the entire conversation. They loved his work and considered him one of the best reporters they had ever had. That was the build-up, before moving onto explaining to him that employment protocol and the new guidelines within the human resources department required him to work office hours and follow protocol. He had failed to do so and had become a 'liability' to the station.

Since he had been let go a year earlier, he had kept up appearances, pretending he wanted to come back to his old job or join any other media station. Truth was, he had made up the story once, thinking it was what society wanted him to say. Ever since, all his former colleagues thought of him as somewhat of a loser who couldn't get another job anywhere. He didn't mind it. The one thing he missed was having a regular pay check, but the freedom he had regained working as a freelancer trumped his need for financial stability.

It was one of the many things he and his now ex-wife had fought about. She wanted a stable, secure and social life, whilst he wanted to chase the truth, no matter how ugly. They had grown apart, each growing into the person they had always been but had hidden in the name of love. Deep down, underneath all the fights, her cruel words and his drinking, he knew he would always love her. She had a power over him he had never understood, she could make him melt with just a simple smile, even after fifteen years of marriage. Many times, he had come home promising himself he would tell her he loved her dearly, and tell her he'd stop drinking. But then she'd pick a fight with him and all his resolutions would fly out the window.

It didn't matter any more. It was over now; he had made sure of that. There was no way they would ever reconcile, and he was finally free to drink as much as he wanted.

He turned his car onto Townmead Road and slowed down. It hadn't been hard to find, as three other police cars with sounds and sirens had driven in the exact same direction. According to his police scanner, they were looking for a woman in her mid-thirties, dressed in traditional Islamic clothing. In his rear-view mirror he saw Channel 4 had also arrived on scene and were slowly driving around with a cameraman hanging out of the window, hoping to get a lucky shot of the action, wherever it was at. It annoyed him not being the only one who had gotten to the site of interest, yet he appreciated their passion for journalism.

As soon as he turned the corner onto the area of Townmead Park, he knew he was in the right place and immediately made what he called an 'inventory of the scene'. Throughout his turbulent, yet successful, career he had spent some years working as a foreign responder. It was during that time he had learned to always screen the scene before setting up. Mainly for safety measurements, but also to get the best shots. Although Townmead Park wasn't anything like a war zone, there was something in the air, and Jack Binckle knew he had to be careful.

The park wasn't very large, but large enough for children to have created a small soccer field out of sticks and bricks showing the side lines, with four small orange pawns which indicated two goals. Two teams of mainly boys, and only two girls, between the ages of eight and twelve, competed as if their lives depended on it. They seemed completely unaware of the danger they had escaped today. To them, the fact their schools had been evacuated and their parents had picked them up in distress, had just turned out to be their lucky day. A day of not having to sit in class.

The children didn't notice the silent sirens, but they were obvious to anyone else in the neighbourhood. Behind each window there was someone watching, uncertain about what they were looking at.

Jack Binckle felt the same way. Townmead Park was surrounded by roads on each side, with houses built in a perfect square around the little park. The fronts of the houses all faced towards the park, and behind the houses were small alleys where bikes were parked and garbage cans would be filled.

Straight ahead, a police car blocked the corner of an alley and the main street. In the far-right corner and on the opposite side of the park, two police cars blocked those entries, too. Only moments after Jack Binckle entered the Townmead Park area, a fourth police car arrived and blocked the final corner. The police officer who had just pulled up behind him, gestured with a serious face for the Channel 4 van to leave and stay outside of the blocked area, unaware another reporter had just successfully entered the barricaded zone.

Moving slowly around the block he didn't quite know what to look for. The neighbourhood seemed rather peaceful, except for the flashlights of the police vehicles. He parked his car behind some others, hoping to blend in and not be asked to leave.

CHAPTER 11

Hello, my beautiful stranger,

Please don't be afraid, just let me speak from my hurting heart.

   The look of the blade...

The way it shimmered in the sunlight, a beautiful sight. I'd almost say I fell in love with it. It just looked so dangerous, yet so loving. The good it could do to my body... it didn't compare to the danger it could do.

It had been on my mind for a couple of days, I loved the idea of people seeing it and realising those were my battle scars, for them to see them as a sign of my strength.

I also loved the idea of it being a way of allowing myself to act as the normal me throughout the day and turn to the knife at night. I wouldn't have to feel guilty for smiling any more because I know I'd feel the pain for it later.

The dangerous touch of that knife, the way it fits into my hand, the way it looks as my reflection stares back at me. I love it, it seems right.

I have no intention of harming myself lethally, I just want to see the blood pour. I want to lick the blood off my skin after I cut. It offers me a sense of relief, as if that tiny opening in my skin allows bad feelings to disappear.

I am in control, although I wonder if I am losing all control at the same time. The more I give in to these voices inside my head, the more creative I become and the more I feel like the real me.

Simultaneously, I also become more cautious of having to hide the real me. I have gone back to drinking and prefer candlelight over the normal lights. I balance between starving myself for days and eating for two on one day.

The look of that blade, the way it fits in my hand, the way my reflection stares back at me.

I know that is and always has been the real me. It doesn't scare me in any way. I believe I am in control. The only thing I am afraid of is the pain. I don't like the pain of the cutting, but the soft burning sensation after is what I have started living for. I plan my cutting, I look forward to it.

I do it in the mornings if I have time, and definitely in the evenings. My obsession grows stronger and more powerful with each day that passes. I am in control for the first time in a long time and I feel like I am getting my powers back.

Throughout the day I am happy, focussed, and driven; exactly how people expect me to be. At night it's me-time, time to let my emotions out. Whether I do that through drinking or cutting, it has to come out some way. It is the path I choose to follow and the further I go, the harder it gets to hide these scars.

Ironically, I don't want to hide them. I am proud of them. They are my battle scars, they are me. Unfortunately, I have to hide the real me again. My true crazy would scare the public.

I've never understood how heroin can be addicting after using it just one time. Now I do. The silver glance of that blade… it has opened up my mind to a new world of possibilities. I believe it makes me high. I could be perfectly sober and still feel as far away from the world as possible when I feel the stinging touch of the knife cutting into my flesh.

It is everything; the way it hurts when I cut and the way the bruises hurt afterwards. But I am most taken by the sight of the cuts when they start to dry. I love the look of those wounds and I feel an urge to perfect them. I can't wait to finish them. I arrange my whole life around being able to cut again, and again, and again. It's like a little painting on my inner wrist, one I need to finish. An ongoing work, a job never done.

The first time I did it, I felt in control. As if I had found some rational way of dealing with pain. But now I am thinking about it continuously, at work, at home, during social events. It is my coping mechanism and scary enough it allows me to cope with things I would have normally considered myself unable to deal with.

Cutting allows me to handle social events better. I tell myself it is okay to be awkward and a bit strange, and now that I am cutting, I find myself acceptive of those characteristics for the first time in my life. Because I know as soon as I go home, I will be piercing that blade through my skin.

That focus, that determination; it has changed everything about my life. My goals have become clearer. And in some way, I think staying away as far as possible from those who are closest to me would allow me to reach those goals without the fear of embarrassment.

I know I hurt people with that logic, but I feel like I deserve to be in pain. The blade serves its purpose and makes me feel all I want and need.

I just can't stop. Everything revolves around it and everything revolves around hiding it. Nobody knows, better yet, nobody has any idea. I know when to cut and where to hide it. I know what to say, how to move and what to wear. I don't want anyone to know, although I fantasise about people finding out and finally realising I am not okay.

I have done it four, maybe five times, but I am addicted. Truth be told, I was hooked after the first time. Hooked on that blade cutting holes in my skin. It is a matter of symbolism to me. All the pain, memories and flashbacks I took in, they were unable to leave me, until now.

Some of these traumas left through tears, which nobody ever witnessed. But a bigger part stayed inside me, digging a hole into my character and soul.

It is as if through those small scratches in my skin, a weight is lifted off my shoulders. It allows me to be happy throughout the day. Strange enough, it allows me to be *me* throughout the day. Because I know, at night, that blade will work wonders for all the bad inside me.

If only I could find somebody to accept my crazy for what it is. If only I didn't have to hide any more.

My love, please don't be afraid —
I've got this under control,
with lots of love from afar, I am thinking of you.

CHAPTER 12

Zahidah ran through the narrow alley behind her house towards the main street. There were exits on both ends, but she had chosen the one on her right side, knowing it was closer to her destination. She knew Rowan had seen her climb the fence and they were now undoubtedly driving towards the crossing of the alley and the main street. Going back to her house was not an option. The sirens came nearer, time was running out for her to escape.

Her maternal instinct told her to return to her children and take them with her. A week ago, she would have never imagined abandoning the two people most important to her. But now, she had no choice. Already having lost one son, it took everything within her to keep on running away from them. Anxiously, she considered her next move. There was only one thing left for her to do, and she grew more paranoid with every second that passed.

Kamal had come to her after the shouting incident, just before he had left the house with the unknown men. He had given her a key wrapped in a small piece of paper. 'Always carry this with you, Zahidah,' he had said. 'I love you.' He had kissed her and gone downstairs to meet the men.

Presuming handling the matter without involving the authorities would be the safest way to go, she had not called the police. Besides, there had been no concrete evidence and it would have meant betraying Kamal's trust. Now, of course, she regretted not having told anyone. If only she could go back in time and change it all. The situation never would have escalated to such a scale.

Tyres screeched over the brick road as Zahidah took another right and ran into the park. The very same park her house could oversee. Her two daughters would often play here, and she could always keep an eye on them through the living room window.

The small playground was too innocent to be surrounded by policemen. No child should have to deal with any of it, especially her very own children. Again, the tyres screeched over the brick road. She quickly looked over her right shoulder and saw a black sedan drive in her direction. It was at that moment she knew she wouldn't make it. But she also realised she could still be an exit for the others.

She stopped running and pulled a gun from underneath her traditional clothing. Walking at a steady pace, she held the gun beside her body and walked into the playground, where about a dozen kids were playing. Some had started noticing something was off and stood silently, listening to the sirens and wondering whether to run or stay put.

Not knowing what was waiting for her, she got down on both knees in the midst of children and said a small prayer, asking for forgiveness and for Allah to protect her children regardless of her sins. She cocked the gun in her hand and stood back up. She was ready to die if necessary.

***

AkQus was established in 1981 and was practically unknown for the first thirty years of its existence. Throughout its first years, the organisation was led by a few powerful men, who were all agents from different international agencies.

Where their superiors would deny other agencies access to certain information due to political issues (read: immaturity), these agents would meet in secret to join their forces and share viable information.

Agents from Mossad, the CIA and Interpol were the first to join, and where the Americans and the Israelis lacked tact, the Europeans would shape an undeniable bond between the two.

The three people who initially founded AkQus had one policy in place which endured nearly all of AkQus' existence: no one was to join unless they were field agents, no one was to become a political dog. It helped them secure the integrity of their organisation, rather than their countries' political interests.

Together they had achieved many admirable goals and prevented wars from happening. However, the war on terrorism between the US and the Middle East grew stronger, and cracks started appearing within AkQus. Europe suffered various attacks, including car bombings and other massacres, leaving many dead or wounded. But Europe was also once again the bond which united AkQus.

Then tragedy struck. The Mossad member died. Of course, with the official channel's communication between the US and Israel on almost zero, the agent's death wasn't reported officially to the US and remained a mystery for quite some time to the other remaining officers.

Right at the start, each founding member had left behind a name in case they were to die. That name belonged to one of their agents whom they vouched for and wanted to follow in their footsteps in becoming their replacement within AkQus should anything ever happen to them.

When a new official within Mossad took over the briefing between Mossad and the CIA, an important document saw daylight which showed the Israeli AkQus agent had died of cyanide poisoning.

By the time the cause of death became known to the two original members of AkQus, it was too late. They had no choice but to trust the man who had entered their secretive ring of intelligence.

After thirty-seven years of AkQus, the two remaining agents were found dead, each in their own apartment only hours apart in their home countries.

The man dressed in black was never heard of again.

***

Zahidah stared at the cars surrounding her. Four of them had created roadblocks, cornering off each escape route. Officers kneeled behind their open doors with drawn weapons.

Standing amidst the laughing and playing children, the panic set in. She looked at the gun in her hand. She did not want to use it here, with these kids around. It was too up-close and personal for her. Children had died in the bombing that morning, too, but for some reason that had not been as hard on her. She hadn't seen their faces right before the bomb had gone off and she hadn't seen them in their school uniforms on their way to a bright future.

A feeling of self-pity and anger came over her. It wasn't her fault. If those men had never come knocking, none of it would have happened. Or at least, their family wouldn't have gotten involved. She had just ended up in this mess against her will. Regardless, now there was no way out.

Looking straight ahead to the SUV parked in the middle of the park, she saw Agent Rowan get out of the car, the engine still running. The door on the passenger side opened and another agent got out of the car. She watched them intently as they slowly walked towards her, holding their hands in the air.

Panic turned into despair and before she knew it, she aimed her gun at the two men. They in their turn, aimed their guns at the woman, shouting from afar for her to put the gun down.

Hoping it would have slowed down the men, she quickly found out it hadn't. They came running at her, from all directions. Weapons drawn, shouting all kinds of orders at her.

The children around her, who had been playing up until a few seconds ago, noticed the change of dynamic and started running in different directions, unsure whether to look at the woman for comfort or run away from all the grown-ups with guns.

In a split second, Zahidah grabbed one of the kids by his jacket and held her arm around his throat, pushing his tiny body against hers. Not in a million years did she think of doing such a thing. There wasn't any other solution. She needed the agents to disappear as much as they needed her to give in.

There was no way back, she knew it. Just a little while longer, a few more memories to pass. A last glance at the house they had called home. Nothing would ever be the same again. She wouldn't feel the pain for much longer, but she knew the wounds on her children's hearts would be there for life. Hoping it was the right thing to do, she tried to control her tears. Another look at that home, her eyes were too watery to see. Hopefully, the female agent kept them away from the window. There was no need for them to see this.

Whispering to herself one final prayer, she had her last glance at her home, ensuring her children did not see it. She released her grip from the little boy and felt him running away from her.

The officers shouted, ran, and barked.

Her eyes closed; a moment of serenity followed. *My children* were the last words which flashed through her mind.

Chapter 13

Our Father in heaven, hallowed be Your name.
Your kingdom come, Your will be done, on earth as it is in
heaven.
Give us this day our daily bread, and forgive us our debts as
we forgive our debtors.
Do not lead us into temptation,
But deliver us from the evil one.
For Yours is the kingdom, and the power and the glory forever.
Amen.

'Hello, Father, I look at myself in the mirror and I find it hard to imagine that the person I have fought to be, is about to go down this dark road again. It's a choice, I know it is. It's a choice I don't take lightly, but also one I can't fight. I have asked You for Your strength and guidance over the past few days, but I can't feel it. I tried, God, please know that.

'The boredom around me, the level of average. I can't stand it. It pisses me off and gives me a headache. I want everyone to leave me alone, but I can't tell them that because everyone thinks I'm doing much better. Only two days ago did someone tell me I'm a lot calmer.

I agreed with her, because in a way I am. But I haven't recovered, I am slipping away again.

'I know You came to me in a dream when I asked You for a sign. You asked me, "What's not going well in your life?" It woke me up in the middle of the night and I realised You were right. Everything in my life has been going increasingly well. Every aspect of my life has improved, as I admitted to You in my prayer that day. And I know it's because of Your support. But that's just it. It's so average, I almost fit in. I don't want to be a part of this group of people. The kind who's fake and unsuccessful. I'd rather be out of it.

'I haven't been able to use the full part of my brain over the past few days. There's this grey area in the middle of my head which seems to be turned off. I don't know what happens there, but I know I am great when it's turned on. I just don't know how to activate it, it's like there's this fog I can't wipe out. It frustrates me because I know I am intelligent, and I wish to do something with that. I just can't when that fog is in the middle of my head. It only ever turns up in the middle, and very rarely in the front. But I think the latter stems from fatigue.

'I try, please know that. I tried the healthy way — praying, writing and exercising. But how long do I have to try this for, before it clears the fog and stops the voices? There's a part of me which is genuinely happy, but there's another part of me which thinks about what it would be like to die. Maybe not die, but disappear. To

be around no one, to just be gone. I ache for that feeling of freedom. To be out of it, maybe just for the afternoon. The problem is, I know if I give myself one afternoon, there'll be more afternoons.

'I hope to be great. I need to clear away the fog for that. I think this is a way to do it. There are tears welling up behind my eyes when I think about the place I am in, once again. But they won't see the daylight, not even when I am alone, because I don't want to feel sorry for myself. I brought this upon me.

'There are three stages. The first one is where I am unhappy and I use it as an escape. Then there's the stage where I recover and fight for stability and happiness. I achieve it, but then I realise I am at risk of being average and nothing in life excites me any more. The beginning of this stage is phenomenal. It's where I know I am getting better, where I am achieving small goals and where I get to be social. But the end of this stage is a place where I feel nothing. Boredom.

'I start seeking for ways to activate this part of my foggy brain, but I can't seem to find it in the daily things. So, I inevitably end up in the same place again; fantasising about cutting and drinking. The fantasising takes over everything. I think about it all the time. Whatever I am doing, there's a voice in the back of my mind. It doesn't necessarily speak to me, but it shows me, pushes me, to where I know I shouldn't go.

'The final stage is my relapse stage. Where I give in and find my moment of happiness. This really is just

a moment; it lasts until I realise I'm a liar and a hypocrite and I don't want to hide any more. That's when I get back to the first stage. And so on.

'Life is boring. And that, to me, is unacceptable.

'I feel so alone... Please give me strength to see me through this.'

In the name of the Father,
The Son,
And the Holy Spirit.
Amen.

CHAPTER 14

'Don't kiss me,' he ordered her.

'I don't want to kiss you,' she reassured him clearly and confidently. 'I just want to be close to you and enjoy your company, because you make me laugh.'

'My head wants you,' he explained, and allowed her to sit on the edge of the coffee table across from him. 'But my body doesn't feel attracted to yours. Not that you're not beautiful… I can't really explain it. I know I am in love with you, or at the very least, I like you a lot.'

'Are you gay?'

'I don't know what I am.'

'I want to touch you with my mind. It makes my heart beat faster.'

She bent her body forward, her head nearly touching his head. He didn't move, he knew she wouldn't try to kiss him.

There was a certain unspoken connection between the two of them. They knew they were it for each other, but they knew it wasn't the time or the place. She was traumatised by some event she hadn't yet explained to him and he had a mission to carry out of course, she had no idea about that. It was on her mind, he could tell. At the same time, he knew he needn't explain it to her.

Society considers cheating to be that of the body only. Where you touch each other and press your bodies against one another. That is cheating. People can get caught doing that. But there's no rule on the cheating of the mind. As long as you don't say the words 'I love you', you can usually get away with it guilt-free.

The problem is: the mind controls the body. He couldn't handle this kind of attention at this time. He needed to be focussed on his mission that lay ahead. He was wasting time, being here, with her. For days he hadn't left his apartment, hadn't watched the news. Even though he tried fighting it every single second every single time, his mind was with hers. He couldn't resist wanting to be around her. The way she looked at him, the way she made him laugh. Her intellect, that was the sexiest thing about her.

'I'm scarred.'

'So am I.'

'I mean mentally. I have… I can't bear physical touch.'

'I have no need for that anyway. But even if I do at some point, I am in no rush. We're intellects in a world filled with common people. We don't need to touch to be satisfied, we don't need violence to convince. The brain is more powerful. I won't touch you, even if at some point I wanted to.'

She nodded her head, her eyes pointing towards the floor.

'I wish you weren't embarrassed about other people's mistakes and foolishness. If anything, you should hold your head up high.'

She looked up, deep into his eyes, their heartbeats synchronising. Their eyes told stories, without the need for words. There had never been a person on this earth who had understood her without having to explain it. She was home.

'It's raining.'

She didn't say it to state the obvious. It was merely a way of saying that the weather suited the situation. The double-shifts had left her feeling exhausted.

When suddenly he had come back into the ER, her heart had skipped a beat. They had exchanged phone numbers and gone out for pizza.

In the back of one of those American-Italian pizzerias, with red-white blocked tablecloths, she had fallen in love with his eyes. Deep, dark brown eyes had looked into hers as if the rest of the world didn't exist. And for a while she had been able to forget the horrors of the hospital. The horrors of the world were shut out by the sound of their synchronising heartbeats.

The pizza had arrived, and they hadn't noticed the appalling atmosphere inside the tiny restaurant. They hadn't noticed the eyes of the owner burning in their direction. It wasn't until he had finally come up to their table and said they were closing, that they had awakened from their daydream at night.

He had paid and they had walked back to his apartment. Never had a city been so awake, yet so quiet.

'What's your name?'

The man dressed in black was startled by the bluntness of the question. The fact each living and dead human being needed a name was beyond him. People were so much more, or so much less, than their name.

'You know mine,' she pressured.

He pondered the possibility of giving her his real name. At some point he was going to be famous. Or infamous, depending on the way you saw things. The visioning of her reaction when she was to find out didn't help him. He hoped she'd be intellectual enough to support his mission, but deep down he knew she might not.

He stroked his hair. 'You mean, you haven't seen my name on the hospital record?'

'No,' she laughed shyly. 'It was so busy… I didn't have time to look at it.'

He smiled at her. 'And here I was thinking you knew me,' he joked.

A smile bounced off her face. Those eyes, he could see his own reflection in them. He questioned whether this was how she saw him. He looked handsome and undoubtedly smart. Perhaps she was ready to know his real name. She wouldn't betray him if she ever did find out about his mission. Not with those smitten eyes of hers.

***

That is the problem with these kind of relationships… there's one person who at some point assumes the other person will be there for them. But finding out they might not be… that is when these beautiful connections break. Love turns into anger. Not because there's no love left, but because the loneliness creeps in. Loneliness… It makes people appear mean.

'I'm not leaving you. I just have stuff I need to sort out, and when I'm done, I promise you, I will be back.' He held his suitcase in his hand.

She didn't want to have to beg for his attention, but she knew how she'd feel after he' left. She was afraid of that feeling. The darkness would find her and absorb her over the next few hours. It would leave her incapable of functioning. Not because she couldn't live without him. No. She was a strong, intellectual woman, but loneliness wouldn't allow her to be herself.

'Fine. Go,' she spoke in an icy voice.

He was surprised by the level of immaturity she portrayed. As if her IQ had dropped. The more she asked him to stay, the more he felt like running out the door and not returning at all. He cared for her, but he couldn't possibly show her. She was troubled, he had a mission.

99

'I will. I will come back when I am done. You can stay in this apartment for as long as you like.'

What others would consider a nice gesture, she considered a bone thrown to a dog. The loneliness had already found her, and he was still here. There was no point in him staying any more. There was simply no coming back from this immature begging. Not today at least. They'd meet again at some point in time and place and they'd have forgotten about this. She would be the strong, independent woman again and he'd be happy to be around her. But what he didn't understand was she couldn't be that version of herself when the darkness took over. She felt nothing in those moments; no need to cry, no need to laugh, no need to function. Total emptiness.

'All right, well, I am going. I need to get to the airport early. I'm not sure if I'd be able to talk to you throughout my trip. I'll be quite busy.'

Even worse… if at least he had given her a time stamp on when she could expect to hear from him, she would have that to look forward to and she could use that to detract energy and motivation to function throughout her daily routine. But no, it felt as if he had hung her out to dry. Her inner strength, what was left of it, told her to pretend to be strong for at least a few words. That might be just enough to have him come back to her at some point.

She hated herself for feeling this way. So dependent on someone else's presence. Her childhood had told her she needed no one to survive all kinds of trouble and trauma. Within her small circle of friends and family, she was one of the strongest. Even she didn't understand her need to have someone near her. Most of the time she was happy to be on her own. Loneliness made her weak. She loathed herself in those moments.

There was just a small light at the end of the tunnel of darkness: the knowledge that the feeling would eventually pass. Whether it would take minutes, hours, days or even weeks. It would pass. But the prospect of feeling nothing but heaviness made her a useless creature. As if she bothered everyone around her with her presence.

'Yeah, no worries.' She forced a smile. 'Have a safe flight and get in touch whenever you're free.' Followed by another fake smile.

The man, dressed in a suit, neat shoes and holding a carry-on luggage, smiled a genuine smile. 'Thank you for understanding.' He walked out the door.

She buried her face behind her hands, embracing her spirit for impact.

CHAPTER 15

Jack Binckle had caught everything on tape. The policemen's shouting, the drawn guns on both sides of the battle and the collapse of the woman's body. They had rushed to her side, guns drawn, as if she had still been able to magically arise and start shooting around with half her brain tissues scattered across the park. One of the agents had rolled her over onto her stomach as another cuffed her lifeless hands behind her back.

Although he had seen his fair share of bloodshed, he had never seen somebody die right in front of him. A shocking sight. It made him angry. He didn't know why, but it was what the way he felt. The young woman had had no chance. Even if she surrendered, her life would have been over. She must have been from around this area and Jack Binckle needed to get to know her better, not just for the scoop but for his own personal peace. The best outcome would be for the woman to have planted this morning's attack. That way he could open up his cold heart and allow himself to not care about her public passing.

Someone around the area would know her name, or even her story. The neighbourhood housed former refugees who had now found a new life in London. It was a quiet neighbourhood, one where the community solved their own problems without involving the police. The tight-knit community had been a victim of an horrendous crime and he knew that many would refrain from talking to reporters. The police would have even less success.

The occupiers of these blocks would be in the news for days as it would now be described and looked upon as a terrorist district. At some point they might even be targeted by riots, claiming that refugees had increased the level of crime in the UK. They would be wrong, but it was a sensitive issue and Jack Binckle had a hunch there was much more to the story than Interpol would lead on.

After a couple of minutes, he was spotted by a woman walking down the road. She was alone and her eyes were puffy red. He pulled over and got out of his car. The woman did not seem keen on his presence, but she also did not run away from him which he considered was a good start. Before he could think of anything to say, she spoke. 'You are the reporter. I saw you with your camera.' The woman spoke good English with a heavy accent.

'That's right.' He paused for a second, thinking of a good way to continue. 'I was hoping I could get her side of the story.'

The woman walked right past him laughing and shaking her head. 'You don't care about us, and no one here will talk to you,' she replied.

Jack Binckle did not like her reaction. She looked down on him. He wanted to give her an arrogant reply but knew it would get him no further. Instead, he decided to take the conversation a different way. 'I have it all on video. The whole thing. I could hand it over and it would be on the news in less than two hours. Or would you like to tell me about her?' He paused again. The look on her face showed him he had hit a nerve. 'What was her name?'

***

Kamal Abadi and his family had fled their home country, Syria, in late 2013 and arrived as refugees in the UK in early 2014. They had never intended on fleeing their home country — they were proud Syrians — but it was the death of Kamal's oldest son that had changed everything.

The airstrikes had reached their home town and Kamal and his wife Zahidah had feared for the lives of their two remaining children, both girls. The Islamic State had forced all inhabitants of their hometowns out of their houses, killing the ones who refused to leave their homes behind.

The Abadi family buried their son, who had turned only sixteen a week prior, in a mass grave. And soon after, they, too, left everything behind.

Together with his wife and children, Kamal had made the most dangerous passage of his life, putting all their savings and his family's future into the hands of human traffickers. Their journey led them from Syria through Turkey overland. A crossing by boat from Turkey to Greece followed, which had been the most fearful moment of the journey, as it was wintertime and the inflatable boat hardly stood a chance on the rough sea waters. From Greece they continued north all the way up to Germany and eventually reached the UK, their dream destination.

***

'So, Laila, where are you from?'

Jack Binckle had taken a seat on the burgundy couch. Across from him, on another burgundy couch, were four young children, staring at him curiously. They were quiet, which made him nervous. In between them was a glass coffee table decorated with candles, coasters and potpourri. Laila had let him into her house and had immediately disappeared into the kitchen to make tea.

'Pakistan,' she answered. 'My husband and I came here with my two children about five years ago. We are British now.'

'You have two children?' Jack Binckle stared back at the four children sitting across from him.

Laila had come out of the kitchen carrying glasses and a teapot. 'Yes, the other two are my sister's.' She put down the teapot and poured him a cup without asking.

He wanted to make a good impression and accepted the tea, although he hardly drank anything else besides coffee and whiskey.

'So, you're watching all the children whilst your husband is at work?' he said, whilst blowing in his tiny teacup.

'No, my husband is dead. He had a heart attack one month after we came here. I live here with my sister and her husband. We take turns watching the children.'

'Ah, okay.' He couldn't imagine three adults and four children living in such a tiny house, but wanted to get back on topic before anyone came home to change her mind.

'What can you tell me about the woman?'

He expected Laila to send the children upstairs before commencing to discuss such a horrific tale, but she sat down in the only free chair and started sipping her tea.

'I will only speak with you if you promise to keep the video outside the news.'

Jack Binckle nodded, although he didn't mean it.

'Her name is Zahidah Abadi. She is from Syria.'

Jack Binckle was glad to have an excuse to put down the tea as he took his notepad out and wrote down her name.

'I do not want to be on the news. It's bad enough my neighbours saw me let you inside.'

'Don't worry. I will leave you out of this,' Jack Binckle reassured her. 'Did she live nearby?'

'Yes.' She pointed to the wall on her right side. 'One street that way. Number 57.'

'Townmead Road?'

She seemed surprised he knew the street name. Hardly anyone knew this area, except the ones living in it.

'Yes. She lives there with her husband and two children. I'm sure they have him, too.'

'They? Who is they?'

'The police, of course. What did you think? That we're not only supposedly housing terrorists but kidnappers, too?'

'No, no, definitely not. I just want to be a hundred percent certain of all the details. What can you tell me about her family?'

'I know she is married twenty-two years this year. They came to London four years ago as refugees. Their oldest son died in a bombing orchestrated by the Islamic State. He was only sixteen.' She took a sip of her tea before continuing, 'They wanted a better life for their children. Most refugees are driven by an instinct to protect their children, it's the basic need any mother or father has. The ones who are filled with revenge don't come here. They stay there to fight. That's why I don't believe Zahidah has anything to do with this.'

It remained silent in the room for a moment. Jack Binckle couldn't imagine any of the four children sitting across from him dying at the hands of any terrorist organisation. Although he wasn't a father, he felt Laila's pain.

'Do you still have a lot of family in Pakistan?'

'Yes, we do. Some of my family don't want to come here. Others are in graves.'

Again, there was a painful silence.

'Your tea is getting cold.'

Jack Binckle picked up the tiny green glass and took a tiny sip. He tried to keep his face from showing disgust, but he was sure Laila had noticed it anyway. One of the younger children giggled and the oldest girl immediately intervened, keeping the kids in line.

Jack Binckle couldn't bring himself to put down the tea again, so he held it in his left hand and wrote with the right.

'What is her husband's name?'

'Kamal. A nice man. Good father and hard worker. They were both doctors in Syria, but the UK government doesn't consider the Syrian degree valid here, so he works as an Uber driver and she works as a cleaning lady.'

Jack Binckle noticed how each time Laila used the present tense when talking about Zahidah, clearly not accepting what had happened.

'Forgive my ignorance, but I wasn't aware Pakistanis and Syrians hung out?'

'It's because you're ignorant we 'hang out' with each other. There's a limited group here in London who understands the traumas we've been through. Zahidah understood mine, and I understood hers. We don't judge each other. We simply want the best for our children.'

'You were friends?'

'Yes, we are. Don't you like your tea?'

Jack Binckle forced himself to take another sip. He knew the conversation was over. He had just one last question before she'd kick him out.

'I thought suicide was considered the highest sin in Islam, yet Zahidah killed herself? She was a traditional Muslim, right?'

Laila stood up. 'Since you don't like our traditional tea, I guess it's best you go.'

'Why did she kill herself, Laila?' Jack Binckle made one last attempt as he grabbed his bag and put the teacup back on the table.

'She did not kill herself. Now, leave my house.'

Chapter 16

Our Father in heaven, hallowed be Your name.
Your kingdom come, Your will be done, on earth as it is in
heaven.
Give us this day our daily bread, and forgive us our debts as
we forgive our debtors.
Do not lead us into temptation
But deliver us from the evil one.
For Yours is the kingdom, and the power and the glory forever.
Amen.

'Hello there, God, there are these dark moments where the silence fills my hope and takes control over my day. It gets so silent inside me I can't even hear the voices any more. It makes me indecisive. Like all guidance has left me, and my will has disappeared.

'In those moments I wish to rely on Your guidance because on those days I am lost, but I can't hear You either. And so I just let the day pass into nothing. Knowing I'll regret throwing away a day You gave me.

'I try to make most of it, but without my personality, the voices, I can't see where I am going.'

In the name of the Father,
The Son,
And the Holy Spirit
Amen.

CHAPTER 17

'Prime Minister.'

He knew not to say much. Patrick had already passed on the message to his secretary, who in her turn had passed it onto the prime minister. All Kneebone had to do was wait for his superior to finish telling him what to do.

Usually, Patrick was the one telling him what to say, but an attack on this scale required someone from higher up the ranks.

'Thank you, Prime Minister.'

He laid the phone back down with a bang. His assignment was simple — don't make Interpol look like a bunch of fools. When asked if Interpol had caught the people responsible, he ought to say 'yes'. 'Don't mention any names, just converse to the media Interpol shot two people dead earlier that day and they planned the attack together,' he had said. None of it was true, but he wanted to keep working for the citizens and pleasing his superiors was the way to do that.

'He said what you would have said,' Kneebone grinned.

'Just another day at the office,' Patrick smirked, as he handed his boss' blazer to him. 'Are you ready or would you like me to stall them?'

'No. We've stalled long enough.'

'Okay,' Patrick said, as he turned around and started moving towards the door.

Kneebone used the reflection of the window to straighten his tie and then walked out into the hallway towards the media room where all the reporters were waiting, or as he liked to call them: *hyenas*.

***

Jack Binckle had just arrived home and immediately turned on his television. He sat down on his worn-down leather couch, placed his bag on the floor beside him and took off his jacket. The channels quickly shifted, some of which showed reports on the bombing, whereas others showed movies or series, pretending that no life-changing event had occurred earlier that day.

He paused at the UK's most popular news channel and was just in time to watch Interpol's director walk out onto the stage. The man seemed nervous, which was unlike his usual television character.

Jack Binckle, without taking his eyes off the television, reached out to a bottle and glass which he had placed on the small coffee table the night before. He poured himself a glass and cussed at himself for spilling some of it. The leather squeaked as he leaned back and waited for Director Kneebone to begin his statement.

***

Kneebone stood in front of a crowd which had more cameras than people in it. The flashes annoyed him, and so he looked down at the blank piece of paper laid out in front of him. Patrick hadn't written him a speech; they hardly ever wrote down what he was intending on saying to the media. Experience had taught them that it made him seem much more insecure to read out each word of the message he wanted to get across.

They had handled the press for fifteen years, but this was the first time he didn't feel completely confident in his PR skills. He would not admit it to anyone, but Alexandra Vanima's presence in *his* town, had made him feel on edge. He hadn't always told the press the truth, sometimes he had blatantly lied, but it had always been for the good of the people. To make them sleep a little better at night, to comfort those who were grieving and to present the strong, united force Interpol wanted to be. This time the lies would be bigger, and he needed to put on a strong front if he wanted the media to believe him.

'Good evening, everyone,' he started, as he looked around.

Those present in the media room immediately quietened down.

'This morning we were the victim of a horrifying attack which occurred at 8.27 a.m. in the Underground at Westminster station. I am sorry to tell you it claimed the lives of forty-seven people.'

He looked back down at the blank piece of paper, hoping it would appear as if he was hiding his emotions of sadness and guilt.

'First and foremost, I want to express my sincerest condolences to those who have lost their loved ones today. I cannot begin to understand your pain and sorrows, the only thing I can do is assure you we have brought those responsible to justice.'

He had tried to make that sound as dominant as he could, but knew something had been lacking in his delivery. He needed to strengthen his statement with details now.

'About fifteen minutes ago, Interpol shot dead two members of the Islamic State, who we know were the masterminds of this shocking attack.'

Now that was a blatant lie, delivered perfectly in such a way, that no one would question its authenticity. The timeline did not match, which meant they could make the suicide of Zahidah Abadi, which had occurred an hour earlier, a side-line of the official investigation. She'd become an unimportant target who had nothing to do with this morning's attack, but had simply been a person of interest in another investigation.

Now it was time to attack the Islamic culture, which would make him favourable with the voters and his superiors.

'The subjects were of Middle Eastern descent and had come to London as refugees about a month ago. We believe they planned the attack in their country of origin, Syria, and they used their refugee status to enter Europe.'

He didn't feel good about what he had just said. Deliberately attacking asylum seekers was beneath him, but if he was to disobey his superiors' orders, they'd have someone else do the exact same. At least this way he could sort of control its magnitude. He took two seconds to gather himself.

Unsure whether there would be an opportunity to ask questions later, a reporter took her chance and asked a question.

'Director Kneebone, was the person who detonated the bomb killed?'

'Yes, the person who detonated the bomb, was a suicide bomber.'

No time to consider his answer. If he did, he'd only create doubt. It was another blatant lie, but they would never find out anyway. Interpol would seal those records and store them as far away from daylight as possible. The way he made it look was that there had been three people involved, and all of them had died within twenty-four hours. A win for Interpol, a loss for immigrants.

Immediately after this question, other reporters started asking questions, too. Kneebone knew this would leave more room for speculation and raised his hand to try and get them to stop. One of the senior reporters, whom he had known for quite some time now, disobeyed his hand gesture, and asked her question anyway.

'Did you include the person who died in the bomb blast in your counting of casualties?'

'No, of course not, Betty. I do not see a reason to name that man in the same group as our beloved citizens. I can hardly consider him a man.'

Before she could ask another question, he continued, 'This terrorist cell included two males and one female, all of whom are deceased. Interpol and local authorities will continue to work together to create a safe environment for its citizens. We will not be answering any further questions at this point. I thank you for your time.'

Kneebone turned away from the cameras and walked out of the media room, ignoring the shouting and orders from the reporters. The doors shut behind him and some of the sound faded away.

He leaned back against the wall. Secretaries and security agents passed by him from the media room on their way back to their level. He needed a moment; he knew this was only the beginning of a long fight to keep his position.

***

Jack Binckle watched in astonishment as Patrick replaced Kneebone' behind the microphone. He held up both hands in an attempt to calm down the reporters, who were now all screaming questions.

'We cannot give you any further information at this time. If there are any new developments, we will let you know. Thank you again for your time.'

Security agents opened the doors at the other end of the room and slowly reporters started moving towards the exit, disappointed with the little information they had gotten.

There was little to no truth behind the statement all of London had waited to hear all day. Sure, Kneebone had addressed the topics which were expected to be addressed, but he had blatantly lied to the citizens of London. There was no way the suspects had all been caught and there was no way any justice had been done within the last twelve hours. The death of Zahidah — that too was a blatant lie.

The more Jack Binckle thought of it, the more it pissed him off. He knew what he needed to do.

***

Kneebone knew his superiors would have wanted him to go harder on the anti-Islamic statements. They had fought a dirty battle with Parliament when more asylum seekers had reached the UK. They simply did not want them in 'their' country.

They had been upset when Parliament had agreed on taking in more refugees and played an even harder battle with their peers trying to get more arrests of those who were of Middle Eastern descent, Muslim, or asylum seekers.

Fact of the matter was that refugees had not coordinated any attack. Not in the UK, not even in Europe. Creating fear within the nation was a great tactic, it could easily influence democratic beliefs. It was why many of Kneebone's peers and colleagues blamed a minority group rather than having faith in a command they helped built.

He closed his office door behind him and poured himself a double Scotch from an expensive bottle he had hidden in his bottom drawer. Years ago, all high-ranking agents had a collection of liquors displayed on little carts in their offices, with expensive glasses to match. But as time progressed, so had the Health and Safety protocols. Eventually, the little carts turned into hidden stashes in bottom drawers. Everyone knew they were there, but out of sight, out of mind, seemed to be the answer.

The alcohol burned as he poured it down his throat. He took out a second glass and poured another double.

Just then, Patrick walked into the office, and gratefully accepted the drink Kneebone held out for him.

Without saying a word, the men sat overlooking the city of London, hoping for a good outcome.

CHAPTER 18

Not wanting to die is one thing,
but having the guts to live
is a whole other level.

'I can't do it.'

'Can't do what?'

'Be normal. I don't last being normal. The first moments always feel like such a relief, like a huge weight is lifted from my shoulders. I can see clearly. Such a relief. I can't tell you, even if you gave me a thousand pages, just how much of a relief it is. But when those moments pass, I just get so uneasy in my own skin. There are these people living inside me and there's just not enough space for all of us.'

'I don't follow?'

'Neither do I... I just can't be normal. And I think sometimes that's exactly what I crave to be most. To be normal. Not to fit in, but to have peace. To have some quiet inside my head, where the voices don't speak.'

'What voices?'

'All of them.' She closed her eyes, painfully aware of their presence within her brain at that moment, too. 'It doesn't just make me depressed or energetic, it also makes me desperate. I can't seem to ever get ahead of them, no matter how hard I try. They're always there and they're always coming back.'

She wanted to cry, but couldn't. There was too much manic energy within her mind, and the only way it could be released was through screaming, laughter or just acting out.

'But they're really voices?' His voice sounded unsure, scared he had met a crazy person.

'I'm not crazy.' She shook her head convincingly, all the while realising it might just create the opposite result.

'I'm not saying you are.'

She shrugged and turned back around. 'They are voices. But not like alter egos, they're me. But not completely myself. Does that make sense?' She turned around to face him and immediately recognised her explanation made no sense to him.

'Are you seeing things, too?'

'Excuse me? What kind of a question is that?'

The blatant question hadn't so much offended her as opened her eyes to the fact he simply had no idea of what it was like to live like her. He was brilliant, yes. Had his own beliefs and opinions, absolutely. But within the field of mental health, he seemed to be ignorantly underdeveloped. A huge disappointment for her, as she could really use some advice.

'I didn't mean to insult you. I just...' He didn't know what else to say. The woman standing in front of him had become a stranger. At first it had all seemed too good to be true. Then again, when it seems too good to be true, it usually is. They had had a connection he had never experienced with anybody else. It had all happened so suddenly and without any effort. They had understood each other without needing a verbal conversation. But since the moment she had told him a little about her weaknesses, she had become more and more of a stranger to him. Not because he liked her less, considered her less beautiful, or thought any less of her, but simply because he didn't understand her.

'Perhaps you aren't the right person for me to talk to.'

The words sounded bitter. They had become that way after the many, many disappointments she had suffered when people she cared about had walked away from her as soon as she had shown her true self more and more.

'No, no. Please, I want to understand you. It's just... I don't get it. You seem like you've got everything it takes to conquer the world.'

He stood close to her now and reached out his hands to grab hers. He hardly ever initiated physical contact. This was more intimate than they had gotten since they had met, standing so closely together as he held both her hands in his.

'I mean, you're intelligent, beautiful, funny. You truly could do anything your heart desires. I don't understand why you would feel the need to run away from yourself…'

'I don't feel the need. It just happens.' Her tone of voice was softer now. She looked at her hands, and her heart beat faster. Secretly, she wanted something to happen, something more. But her brain didn't want it, her brain needed something else. It needed to be understood by the man who she had fallen for. He had asked for an explanation and seemed patient enough to want to listen to it. But it wasn't the first time she had gotten this opportunity, may it be from different people, it had always failed.

Failed because the reality wasn't as fun and loving or calm and caring as the person she was on the outside. Although she was that person on the inside, too, within herself there was something else completely. Something she couldn't hide when she would be around the same person for longer periods of time.

'What do you mean, it just happens?'

'I mean to say, I can't control it… It takes me. No matter how hard I fight it, no matter how much I don't want it to happen. It comes, without any kind of warning, and just completely takes over everything. When I get down.' She slipped her hands out of his, walked a couple of steps back and turned her back on him. 'I don't just get down. I get depressed. Truly depressed. And you can tell me anything you'd like; it may be the weather, hormones, past trauma's, or anything else. But please don't, because deep down I know the truth. And I think you do, too… I think we both know the reality is I suffer from episodes of depression.'

She turned around to face him again, expecting him to just stand there, unsure what to do. Before she knew it, his lips touched hers.

CHAPTER 19

Jack Binckle sat at his desk in his dark apartment. He had moved there after his divorce and done next to nothing to decorate it. Spending most of his time writing or reading, he had furnished the living room with a large desk, a three-seater sofa — often used as a bed when he drank too much — and a large cabinet stacked with books. His desk was the messiest place of the house, which he loved. He couldn't work on a neat desk, he needed chaos to write. Another characteristic which hadn't complied with the new HR guidelines. According to them, the office needed to look professional so it would create a safe and warm environment for everyone.

The stacks of books, magazines and newspapers made him feel at home. The laptop placed amidst the organised chaos was the only source of light in his apartment, besides the moon shining through the two large windows located in the living room and the open-plan kitchen.

The video of Zahidah Abadi committing suicide would be more than enough for a big pay-out, but he wanted more than that — to embarrass Director Kneebone. It had been a while since he had truly investigated a story, and his gut told him this would be the right time for him to get back in the game. Knowing he had the best footage and source, he brooded over a plan to be able to control the article.

Footage like this did not come about every day and it would make most of the citizens of London ecstatic to see a terrorist die on the screen. He could sell the video and at the same time demand to be the one to write the article. There was a possibility he could even have his name printed on the article.

Jack Binckle did not have much faith in governmental organisations, or perhaps he was just a paranoid reporter who only saw the negative side of things. People, especially governmental employees, would do insane things to sell more papers. Thinking no one would ever find out the truth anyway or paying off the ones who came too close to it.

He put his drink down and started rummaging in his desk drawer, looking for a business card. He hesitated shortly and then dialled the number.

'Meggie?'

'Oh my God, Jack? How have you been?' She sounded sincerely surprised, but friendly as always.

'I'm good. How have you been?'

'Yeah, I'm great. I'm in charge of the editorial department now.'

She sounded happy and he did not want to mess with that, nor did he want her to ask more about his life. So, he decided to cut the chit-chatting short.

'Good on you. Listen, I've got something I think you will be interested in.'

'Oh, I'm not sure, Jack. Last time you said you had something interesting, you nearly broke the window in my boss' office.'

'This is not that. Trust me, this is worth every second of your time.'

'Okay… but I prefer to not meet in the office. How about we have a drink at our old spot in an hour?'

'See you there. Thanks, Meggie.'

'I hope I'm not making a mistake agreeing to meet with you, Jack.'

Without comforting her, he hung up, finished his drink and got to work on his article.

CHAPTER 20

Choosing safety meant confessing and admitting I was weak.

She was alone. Her reflection looked tired, pale even. She was in no mood to take a shower, but she knew she'd feel better after. The mirror on the inside of the bathroom door caught her undressing herself. First her sweater and shirt, then she loosened her belt and unzipped her pants.

Still wearing her matching black underwear, she stood in front of the mirror and watched herself. Nothing appeared to be wrong with her; the bracelets on her left wrist covered a horror story only she knew of. It still surprised her how easy it had been to hide. People would pay her compliments on her bracelets or watch, not knowing she used them merely as a decoy.

She took off the colourful, innocent pieces of jewellery and placed them on the sink. The small white lines looked flawless. She picked up the small blade she had already laid out on the sink and sat back down in the chair. It made her smile, happy even, to watch herself in the mirror as the blade got nearer to her wrist. Her heart filled with joy as it pounded away loudly. She bit her lower lip, still smiling, and put the blade back down. She walked over to the bathtub, set the plug and ran the water. This was a moment worth savouring.

In the kitchen, she grabbed some green tea bags, chamomile tea bags and sliced up some cucumber. She placed it all onto a cutting board and threw it into the steaming water. Then she undressed further and stared at her naked body. Some parts she admired, other parts she loathed.

Knowing the relief would soon be with her, she stepped into the warm water, tightly clutching onto the blade in her right hand. Her body relaxed as she leaned back and searched for tea bags with her left hand. Momentarily, she placed the blade on her stomach, where it floated a little into the water and landed back onto her stomach each time she drew a breath.

Tea dripped over her face as she squeezed it out of the bags. This was a moment of relaxation. In the bedroom, through the door she had left slightly open, she could just see the TV. An old-fashioned movie was on. She hadn't followed it, but the old English accents in the empty and lonely motel room were reassuring. She closed her eyes for a few seconds and tried to reach that moment of absolute relaxation. She couldn't. She couldn't until, and she knew that.

Without even opening her eyes, she found the blade and held out her wrist. Only then did she look at what she was about to do. The most peaceful moment of her day.

An old line reopened.

CHAPTER 21

I didn't not cry because I didn't care.
I didn't cry because I wanted to not care,
I didn't cry because I felt such intense sadness,
I couldn't cry any more.

It had been a short night. Everyone had been busy trying to find links and processing evidence from the crime scene. Flynn had been glued to his computer screens for at least sixteen hours when Curtis had summoned him to go home and get some rest. He had protested a little but gone anyway, relieved he could get some sleep, as he knew a good night's rest would be only a dream, at least for the next few weeks.

After sending Flynn home, Curtis had told the rest of his team to go home, too. It was nearly two a.m. and they had not gotten any closer to understanding why Zahidah and Kamal Abadi had wanted to attack London. Nothing in their personal life had suggested they were involved with terrorists, not here in London and not back home in Syria. Although of the latter they weren't a hundred percent sure, as the communication with the English embassy in Syria was, to say the least, challenging. Most embassies had been vacated and the personnel had been evacuated back to London as the Islamic State had gained more and more territory. Some had stayed behind, but those were agents, and their goal was to survive day by day whilst attempting to gain more intel.

It was seven a.m. sharp and the Interpol team had just gathered again in their office. Curtis was feeling rather strange about the whole case. Zahidah's suicide simply did not add up. Unsure how to start and not wanting to jump straight in, he decided to ask his team a question which had kept him up almost all night.

'If there was a God, why would He allow this to happen?'

Edmonds and Rowan looked at each other, unsure how to handle the question. Eventually, Edmonds spoke up. 'I don't really believe there is a God... I was raised Catholic, but I don't practice it any more.'

The awkward silence returned as Curtis took her answer into consideration. Neither had ever heard Curtis bring up religion; it was a sensitive topic within Interpol. Some agents had adopted tunnel vision throughout their experience at Interpol and blamed the first Islamic suspect they could find. Other agents, like Curtis and his team, were more tactful and always opted for a fair investigation.

'Why do you ask?' Rowan attempted to get something out of Curtis.

'Because I don't believe any religion would want this,' he said, as he pointed at the pictures of the crime scene.

Forty-seven. They were sitting in their unit's office. Each unit had their separate offices, theirs being located at the corner, with big windows overlooking sombre London.

'I'm with you on that,' Edmonds agreed. 'No religion would want children to die on their way to school...' She found it hard wanting to sound professional but also showing her emotions at the same time.

'All right. So, let's summarise,' Curtis decided to get started. 'We've got forty-seven casualties and one in the ICU.' He spoke emotionlessly in an attempt to detach himself from the horrifying crime that had been committed. Then he shifted his gaze from the pictures on the whiteboard filled with evidence and 'leads' back to his team. 'Did you find Jane Doe's bag?'

'Yes, we did,' Edmonds answered, 'but it was completely blown up, so we haven't been able to use any of it to identify her.'

'Are we sure she is a victim?' Rowan asked.

Having spent nearly fifteen years in the field, he knew to trust no one until after they were proven innocent. The law may have said 'innocent until proven guilty', but his investigative nature worked just the other way round — guilty until proven innocent.

'She's not in any way involved. I vouch for that personally.' Curtis rubbed his hands together as he leaned back into his chair at the head of the table. 'But,' he continued, 'I do agree with you that her presence at the scene at that time and being the only survivor calls for many questions.'

'You vouch for her personally? You know her?' Rowan stood by his initial questioning.

'Let's call it my gut instinct, Rowan.' He gave his agent a stern look. 'What else?' Curtis glanced over to Edmonds, knowing she was eager to speak about everything she had learned.

Edmonds gave a quick nod and then stood up. 'Well, according to the preliminary reconstruction forensic gave us, the staircase indeed saved our Jane Doe's life. Past experiences have told us that suicide bombers wear their bombs on their bodies, not in a briefcase, and ninety-nine percent of the time they die. If she was involved, then she would be a really dumb bomber,' Edmonds explained, and handed the preliminary report to Rowan.

'Also,' she continued, 'the fact all other persons of interest in this case are of Middle Eastern descent, and the fact she is Caucasian makes it unlikely for her to have been involved.' She looked at Curtis.

'Unlikely, but not improbable,' he replied. 'But you're right. If she was involved, she would have been as far away from that place as possible. It's a miracle she didn't die, though...' He looked at the pictures again. The dead bodies were unrecognisable. So far, they'd only been able to identify six of them, they had been the only ones who had resembled some of the identity cards they'd found in the debris.

Throughout the morning they would allow families to come into the morgue and have a look for themselves. Interpol had never before allowed families to come into the morgue on such a scale, but Curtis' superiors considered the agony of not knowing whether their loved ones had died the previous morning far greater than looking at severely injured corpses.

Curtis thought the whole thing was incredibly horrendous. Some might find what they were looking for only to realise that it was not at all what they were looking for.

'How did you get this report?' Rowan asked.

'I went past the forensic lab yesterday on my way home.'

She did not mean to sound like the most diligent agent in the room, but she knew Rowan would take it as a personal insult for trying to outsmart him. Although that had not at all been her intention, she felt a need to make up for a mistake no one had accused her of; it was her negligence which had allowed Zahidah to escape. And because of that, their only lead was now dead.

'Hmm…' was all he replied as he continued to read the report.

'On top of that, the man Flynn showed you yesterday on the surveillance tapes has not been found in the debris. There's no one in the morgue matching someone with his height, weight, build or Middle Eastern features. There's a possibility he's still out there,' Edmonds spoke again.

'Yep.' Curtis sighed deeply. 'There is a possibility he is still out there. And the only description we have is that of a man which can fit thousands.' Curtis chuckled out of despair.

'What about the residue found on the parts of the briefcase found at the crime scene?' he asked Edmonds.

She had an interest in the forensic side of things. The only thing she did not like about it was sitting inside all day long, which is why she had opted for the police school rather than science at some fancy university. She was the quietest, but worked harder than anyone else in the anti-terrorism unit. As the only female she did not want to be considered a 'liability', something some agents felt women in the field to be from time to time.

Luckily, neither Rowan nor Curtis considered her a liability. But they were protective of her, more so than they may have been with a male agent. In an effort to stand out for her skills rather than for painting her nails, she was the first one in and the last one out. If Curtis summoned her to go home and get some rest, she'd take home the files and read them in bed whilst watching the news.

'It's still being tested. So far, forensics have found traces of C4, which is not surprising. They're trying to determine the type of leather the briefcase was made of.

That way they can narrow down the branding and perhaps uncover at which store it was bought.'

'That's a one in a billion shot,' Rowan filled in hopelessly.

'Guys! I need you to come see this immediately,' Flynn said, as he stormed into the unit's office.

Before anyone could reply, he had already turned around and was on his way back to his own office. Curtis, Edmonds and Rowan followed him hastily down the hallway through the common room, which was still hosted by agents from different agencies and had turned into a chaotic sight with files, empty drink cartons and leftovers in food containers. When they arrived at his office, Flynn was already sitting in his chair. He pulled up one chair for Curtis and pointed at one of his screens.

'We were able to restore some of the video footage,' he said. Not in the least did he try to hide his excitement, knowing he had just made a breakthrough in the case.

Curtis looked at Flynn and smiled. 'That's great. Finally, some good news.'

'Now, the image is somewhat distorted, but I'm afraid it won't get any better than this.' He pressed play and pointed at the white Prius pulling up at the Underground's entrance. 'That's Kamal Abadi, our Uber driver. As you can see, his passenger hands him something, we don't know what, and forensics did not recover it from his car.'

Everyone looked at the images intensely.

'Here he is getting out of the car with the briefcase and entering the Underground. Then we lose him for a little bit, but another camera picks him up again about thirty-seven seconds later.'

He closed the window of the first footage and opened a second one. 'Do you see it?'

'Platform six. Ground zero...' Curtis replied.

'Same man, same briefcase,' Rowan replied.

'Or at least a man with the same description. Can't be a hundred percent sure... The footage is too distorted,' Edmonds replied.

'All we could get out of it, Edmonds,' Flynn replied, a little offended. Again, he closed the window and opened another.

'This footage is from platform six, but from a different angle. We were able to reconstruct a few seconds of the footage right before the bomb going off. Now wait for it.' He pressed play, and waited for the video to finish.

'You see that woman?'

Curtis stared at the footage. He had put his reading glasses on as to not miss a thing. 'That's her... Play it again, but in slow motion.'

Flynn did as he was told and ran the same footage times 0.25 speed.

Curtis got closer and watched as the guy with the briefcase walk onto the platform right onto the spot where one of the Underground train's' doors would open upon arrival. Then, as if someone calls out his name, he suddenly looks to his left and starts moving towards the woman.

The woman, whose face isn't caught on camera and who's standing beside the stairwell, at first doesn't notice his presence. But as he gets closer, her body language turns to that of a statue. As he keeps walking towards her, she walks away from the railway and to the back of the staircase, briefly showing her face — enough for Curtis to conclude it's her.

'That's the end of the footage. I'm afraid that's as much as we'll get out of it.' Flynn pressed pause and turned to Curtis.

Curtis nodded. 'She saw him.'

CHAPTER 22

'In the studio with us today is Jack Binckle, a former reporter for *The Times*. Jack, what can you tell us about yesterday's statement made by Interpol's director, Wayne Kneebone?'

Jack Binckle didn't like the 'former reporter for *The Times*'-reference. To show that, he paused for a moment, looking sharply into the newsreader's eyes, a young guy with too much self-tanning product on his face. He had probably never spent a day in the field, but was still entrusted with bringing the news to the nation. It made Jack sick to his stomach.

'Jack?'

'Yes. I believe yesterday's statement is false. A woman died yesterday, she is believed to have ties to the terrorist cell responsible for the Underground attack, but she wasn't terminated by Interpol. She committed suicide.'

'Well, does it really matter whether she was shot or committed suicide? I mean, the point is that she's dead. Am I right?'

'No, you are not right,' Jack Binckle answered shortly, becoming infuriated with the newbie.

He clearly had no idea what the job of a real reporter entailed, so he shifted his focus from the newbie newsreader and looked straight into the camera.

'Interpol has lied to you about last night's events. I was there when Zahidah Abadi turned the gun on herself and died. It was around four p.m. yesterday, not five-forty-five p.m. as Interpol likes you to believe. If we cannot trust what's being said about this event, how can we be sure that there aren't still members of the cell on the loose?

'I believe they are playing dirty politics. The fact is, nobody knows who is responsible for yesterday's attack. Director Wayne Kneebone said two males and one female allegedly planned the attack. Interestingly enough, Zahidah Abadi's husband Kamal Abadi hasn't been seen or heard of since the bombing. Is he the one Interpol was referring to? And if so, is he really dead or are they holding him in a bunker somewhere whilst they're torturing him because they're afraid of more attacks? All I'm saying is, I believe that us citizens have a constitutional right to know what happened to our loved ones. Director Wayne Kneebone, Interpol, if you're listening: we want the truth!'

'Okay… Thank you, Jack.' The newbie newsreader spoke hesitantly as he looked back into the camera. 'Moving on. A memorial service will be held tomorrow at ten a.m. It is believed Director Kneebone and members of parliament will be present.'

The sound of his voice faded away as Jack walked towards the exit. He knew he'd be followed by Meggie and he knew she'd be pissed. He quickly walked down the hall, hoping he'd be gone by the time she'd appear.

'Jack!'

He kept walking.

'Goddamn it, Jack! You promised you wouldn't make me look like a fool.'

He stood still and spun around.

'You can't keep pulling shit like this on me, you know. You could get me fired. Or is that what you want, huh? Payback for what happened to us?'

'Happened to *us*? As I see it, you've gotten yourself another job and I'm the one trying to make ends meet. But it's become quite clear to me that you've exchanged your integrity as a reporter for a pay check.'

He looked at her and let the words he just spoke sink in. He hoped to get a reaction from her, for her to hit him or yell at him. Instead, she just stood there, quietly watching the tips of her shoes.

'You never had the balls to make it anyway.' He turned back around and walked out the sliding door.

***

There seemed to be no way out. Every move he might make, would put him in danger of losing his job. Jack Binckle had made sure of that. If anyone was going to reveal Jane Doe's identity, it would be him.

The odds of former Special Agent Alexandra Vanima being the sole survivor seemed too extraordinary, even for someone with her past. The likelihood of it all being a coincidence seemed to be non-existent. But that left only one other option: she was involved in some way. Either way, it was a PR nightmare.

He sighed and put the empty glass down on his desk. It was too early to drink, but time hadn't stopped him. He opened the drawer and took out his favourite. The bottle smelled like comfort. Instead of pouring another one, he drank the burning drink straight from the bottle.

He looked at his reflection in the window. A middle-aged man in an expensive suit, drinking straight from the bottle, feeling sorry for himself. He walked over to the window and looked through it, down to the world beneath him.

Down there, someone had created a horrible mess which he now had to clean up. The street was still locked down, but it hadn't stopped people from placing hundreds of candles, flowers and teddy bears. Only yesterday morning the world, his world, had been a different place. He longed to go back.

No way out. Yet, he felt strangely calm. Perhaps it was because he knew it was over, perhaps it was because his sixth sense told him that there'd be an escape route for him somewhere.

He needed a fresh pair of eyes and decided to walk down to get some air. He grabbed his blazer and shut the door behind him. With a quick gesture, he summoned Patrick to follow him.

Quickly, Patrick ended his phone conversation and jumped into the elevator just before the doors shut.

'Fresh air?'

'Parking garage.'

'Good idea,' Patrick agreed, as he pushed the B1 button.

The elevator moved them quickly past twelve floors, without letting anyone enter their brainstorming session.

A soft ding and a female voice announcing they had arrived at 'level B1' made Patrick speak up.

'How about some gambling tonight?'

'Sounds exactly like the type of distraction I need.' Kneebone smiled. 'But first, I want to pay someone a visit.'

***

Jack Binckle had just returned home from the studio. The internal struggle he had had with himself during the taxi ride home had left him drained. He was proud of what he had done on air, but he felt rather guilty for lashing out at Meggie. As he opened his laptop, he decided to refrain from feeling bad about the situation.

He had saved her career before whilst his had taken a fall. He had repaid her more than he ever should have.

The problem was, now he had lost on-air time in the studio. Then again, when other channels saw what he had dared say on camera he might have a shot getting with one of them. His inbox showed no new emails had arrived just yet. Maybe he was too eager too soon.

He longed for a good, few hours of sleep, but knew he needed to have more evidence and details in case someone was to respond to his outburst.

He got up, walked into the kitchen and brewed himself some coffee. As the coffee maker did its job, he thought of his next move.

Chapter 23

Our Father in heaven, hallowed be Your name.
Your kingdom come, Your will be done, on earth as it is in
heaven.
Give us this day our daily bread, and forgive us our debts as
we forgive our debtors.
Do not lead us into temptation,
But deliver us from the evil one.
For Yours is the kingdom, and the power and the glory forever.
Amen.

'Hello there, God, at times I feel very lonely as I go along on this journey of sobriety and self-love. No one around me seems to know the battles I'm fighting. Even though some are aware of my past and my demons, they don't seem to understand these demons haven't disappeared along with the bottles of alcohol and knives.

'I wish I had someone to talk to besides You. Forgive my boldness, but it would be nice to face someone from time to time. Someone who's there physically, not just in spirit.

'I know You're always here for me, because I have felt Your presence. But over the past couple of days

Your presence seems to have become more distant. I think it's because of him, you know who I mean. I care for him deeply, but I know being with him is a form of self-harm. You know the pressure I was under and the coping mechanisms I resorted to. I don't want to go back down that path again.

'I'm a huge believer of following your heart, but I know this isn't my healthy heart talking. My dark heart aches for drinking and cutting and, I know now, it isn't the right instruction to follow.

'I ask of You to guide me and to please show me You haven't distanced yourself from me. I need You; I don't want to relapse. Please help me.'

In the name of the Father,
The Son,
And the Holy Spirit.
Amen.

CHAPTER 24

The more I try to become
cold-hearted,
the less I feel
like I am.

'So, whereabouts?' Edmonds asked.

'Right here.' Brian pointed at the middle of the playground.

As Edmonds got closer, she noticed the blood on the once grey playground tiles.

'I'm surprised nobody has cleaned it. I figured their adversity towards us may have been care for her, but I guess I was wrong.'

She kneeled down and had a closer look at the tiles. She tried to imagine being Zahidah as if to understand what went through her mind. She had seen horrible things in her time as an agent. But someone blowing their own brains out was a new one. She'd usually have to deal with violence against her and her colleagues, not talking people off the ledge or, in this case, to move their weapon away from their own head.

She'd been shot herself. The terrifying moment still haunted her at times when she was trying to fall asleep.

She was glad she hadn't witnessed this particular incident, but refused to let it show around the men in her unit, and in this case Brian.

'All right. So, she was standing here.' She got back up. 'Where were you?'

'Over there.' Brian pointed behind her.

'Okay. Rowan and Curtis on the other side, yes?'

'Well, yes. But I don't see the need to re-enact the damn thing. I mean, we were here. She killed herself.'

Edmonds shaped her right hand into a gun and put her index finger against the right side of her head.

'Right-handed, yes?'

'I guess so.' Brian was unsure of Edmonds' point.

'Okay, get into your position and pretend to hold out your gun.' Brian did as he was told and walked about ten metres behind her, pretending to be holding a gun.

Edmonds, still holding her index finger against her head, slowly started spinning around. 'Tell me where I was standing, precisely.'

'Little bit more to your right and facing Curtis' car.'

Edmonds took two steps away from the bloody tiles and faced the place where Curtis and Rowan had been the day before.

'What's the point in all this, Edmonds?' Brian shouted.

She ignored him and squeezed her eyes, feeling the curious eyes of neighbours burning in her back. She dropped her fake gun hand and walked away from Brian towards the street.

He got up and followed her. *Women*. He hadn't the faintest idea what was going through her mind and was starting to get increasingly more uncomfortable. In each house at least one person was staring at them, but when he gave in and looked back, the only thing he saw was curtains moving.

Edmonds had stopped walking and now pressed her face against one of the windows.

'What in God's name are you doing?' Brian was starting to get fed up with her odd behaviour.

'Every single person in this block is watching us.'

'I'm well aware,' Brian murmured under his breath.

'Everyone except this house. Look.' She urged him to press his face up against the window, too.

Brian pressed his nose against the cold window and tried to see as much as he could past the semi-open curtains.

'Looks like someone has left in a hurry.'

'Exactly. I'm calling Curtis. We need forensics to do a full sweep.'

'You won't be able to get a warrant just because nobody is watching your strange act in the middle of the block.'

'We're dealing with terrorists. We don't need a warrant, suspicion is enough,' she said as she dialled his number. 'You stay here. I'm going around the back. See if there's something interesting going on there.'

Edmonds reached the backyard and pushed against the fence, which to her surprised wasn't locked. She had a look around the alley and put her right hand on her gun. Slowly, she started moving inside and cleared the garden, noticing the back door being ajar. She took her gun out of its holster and held it alongside her body as she pushed the door open. It gave a soft creaking noise.

She pointed her gun up and entered the house. The first room she entered was the kitchen, which she realised was going to be a forensic nightmare. There were empty food containers, leftovers, dirty dishes and pans everywhere. As she moved through the kitchen, she also noticed a smell growing more intense the closer she got to the living room door.

Experience had taught her the meaning of that smell, one she'd never forget. She pushed the door open and immediately covered her mouth, gagging. A body had been hidden from the living room window and dragged behind the couch. Maggots covered the body's mouth and nose. She continued down the room towards the front door. When she was certain the downstairs was clear, she opened the front door as quietly as she could.

An unaware Brian was waiting on the other side of the front door, growing more agitated by the crowd watching him with each second that passed. The turning of the lock startled him, but he was relieved to see Edmonds on the other side of it. Even before Edmonds spoke, he had one hand covering his mouth and the other grasping his gun.

'Downstairs is clear, except for the body I found,' she whispered.

'No shit. Let me call for back-up.'

'No, upstairs. Now!' Edmonds was the first one on the stairs, both hands on her gun, pointing towards whatever might come their way.

On the top of the stairs, she gestured Brian to take the left two bedrooms as she herself took the bathroom and the toilet. Everything was clear.

'Now we call it in.' Edmonds said as she dialled Curtis' number again and walked downstairs to the body.

'Ah, shit. The smell is fucking horrific,' Brian complained.

'Not picking up.'

'Are you calling Rowan?'

'Hmm, sure,' Edmonds said as she dialled.

'You don't like him very much, do you?'

'On the contrary. I think he is a great colleague,' Edmonds said as she kneeled down next to the body. They had been careful not to step in any of the blood residue or to touch any of the surfaces.

'Hi Joan,' Edmonds spoke into her phone. 'We've got a body. Ellis Street number 65.' She paused for a second as she waited for an ETA. 'Great, see you then.' She closed the call and dialled Rowan. As she waited for him to pick up, she ordered Brian to call forensics.

'Edmonds?' Rowan spoke loudly.

'We've got a body. If you're not busy come down to Ellis Street, number 65, next to where Zahidah was shot.'

'Where she killed herself, you mean. I'm on the way. Call the forensic team and don't touch a thing.'

'I've already called forensics.' She hung up without saying anything further and gave Brian a stern look, which warned him from saying anything.

'Go grab some mouth masks, shoe covers and the camera from the car,' she ordered Brian.

She took a pair of gloves out of her jeans and put them on. No matter where she was, she always stacked at least one pair in her jeans, even on her days off.

Brian nodded and walked out of the room as he gave the forensic team the address. Now that everyone had been alerted, Edmonds had a moment to herself to inspect the corpse lying in front to her. The body was a male who appeared to have been in his late thirties or early forties. His Middle Eastern facial features showed slight wrinkles and his hair had started growing grey at the sides. He seemed to be in good condition, apart from the bullet wound in his head.

'Forensics will be here in twenty minutes, depending on traffic.' Brian spoke with a muffled voice as he put covers over his shoes. He had already put his face mask on and gave the other one to Edmonds, who gratefully accepted. 'So, what do you think?'

'Fired from close range, execution-style.'

Brian nodded and put his gloves on as he stood in the door opening of the living room. He got away from the body and started looking through some papers lying on the table. He wasn't a newbie, but the maggots made him sick to his stomach and he needed a second to get used to the idea.

'I think he's been dead for at least a day or two.'

'So… before Zahidah, then.'

Edmonds did not reply. It annoyed her when people asked for a confirmation of the obvious. She picked up the body's hand and realised rigor mortis had already set in. Carefully, she turned it over to get a closer look at his fingers.

'Fuck. His fingerprints are covered in scars.'

'What?'

'Take a look.'

Brian came closer and tried hard to keep himself from gagging.

'You see? Somebody burned of his fingerprints. Judging by the scarring, it was done some time ago. Maybe he was in our system.'

'So, we won't be able to identify him this way,' Brian thought aloud. 'What about his teeth?' They shared a look of disgust. Neither one of them wanted to put their hands near maggots, but Edmonds also knew it had to be her. She couldn't appear weak, especially not in front of Brian. Edmonds replaced the hand the same way she had found it and put her fingers between his lips. She felt the maggots crawling over her gloves and tried to keep her eyes on the teeth. She would have preferred to run out the door and take a long shower, but she wouldn't have her image tainted.

'I'm not sure. He seems to have perfect teeth, or they're fake ones.'

'Joan should be able to let us know.'

'Yep.' She sighed with relief as she pulled her hand back and changed the subject. 'Anything in those papers?'

'Newspapers and commercial flyers. There is a number on it though, and maybe fingerprints.'

'All right. Take pictures of everything and then start digging into every single inch of this place.'

'You got it.'

Brian turned on the camera, dangling from his neck, and started taking pictures of the bloody dragging marks. Then he took pictures of the body itself as Edmonds waited for him to finish.

'Make sure you get a close-up of his head. There's no visible gunshot residue on his head, so perhaps the killer used something as a silencer.'

Brian did as he was asked and shot the close-up. He was still disgusted by the maggots, but through the lens it seemed as if they were farther away.

Edmonds looked around the room. There was hardly any furniture. Except for the two couches, a table and a few wooden chairs, the room was empty.

'We should question the neighbours. They must have heard something. At the very least, they'd be able to give us a description of the residents. Although, I doubt they'll talk.'

Brian had finished photographing the body. 'It's a long shot. Then again, if we can link this death to terroristic activity, we can force them to speak.'

Edmonds got out her phone again. 'We have got to call more back-up and bring in the neighbours. If we wait, they might flee.'

Brian nodded and walked over to the table, where he took a picture of the number written on one of the commercial flyers. The number was two digits longer than a regular number, and before he could start thinking about what that could mean, there was a knock on the door.

'Darn it. The smell,' was Rowan's first comment as Brian let him into the house.

Edmonds had just finished her phone call and proceeded to bring Rowan up to speed. She ended her monologue by asking him whether he had been in touch with Curtis.

Rowan shook his head and kneeled down next to the body. 'Is he carrying anything on him? ID or anything else?'

'I was just about to search his pockets.'

Rowan had covered his shoes and put on gloves, but he wasn't wearing a mouth mask, which made Edmonds wonder whether she should take hers off. Then again, if she took it off now, she'd look like an idiot for wearing it in the first place. So she left it on.

The dead male was wearing dark jeans, a pair of sneakers, a t-shirt and a leather jacket, but a search of the pockets revealed nothing.

'How about any tattoos?' Rowan suggested, and he moved closer to the body so he could pull up one of the jacket's sleeves.

'Be careful. Rigor mortis has already set in.'

It annoyed Edmonds that he was taking over the search of the body she had found. If it hadn't been for her, nobody would be here now. Nevertheless, she stripped up the sleeve on 'her' side of the body and found a partial tattoo. It was obvious the man had tried to get rid of the tattoo with laser treatment, as it had started to fade, but hadn't been able to finish all treatments necessary to completely remove the tattoo.

'What does it look like?'

'Not sure. I guess it's some Arabic writing with some sort of a symbol underneath it. He's undergone laser treatment to remove it. I suppose he needed to get one more to completely get rid of it.'

'How do you know how many treatments it takes?' Rowan asked with a grin. 'Experience?'

Edmonds chose to ignore his childish comment, although she felt like slapping his face. Another knock on the door gave Edmonds an opportunity to walk away, hoping it was Joan.

Joan was Interpol's medical examiner. A direct woman with more field experience than most of the agents, and not to be messed with. Intimidated by her knowledge, most agents would stay away from her as she did her preliminary field examination. Edmonds had learned a lot from Joan and was always the one to volunteer when things needed to be picked up from the morgue. Joan knew she had a thing for the forensic side of Interpol's investigations and allowed her to come down to her office to discuss certain matters in great detail.

'Edmonds! My assistant is busy at the morgue, so you'll have to do.'

'Not a problem.'

Edmonds was relieved she was in the presence of a great woman, and it immediately gave her a confidence boost.

'Brian. Go get the gurney from my van, will you.'

Brian immediately put his camera down and walked out the door.

'Rowan, I hope to God you haven't touched something you're not supposed to be touching.'

'No, no. Of course not,' Rowan replied, and gave Joan a faint smile. 'I'll continue taking photographs. So that you can assist Joan,' he told Edmonds, who replied with a sarcastic smile.

'Don't touch anything!' Joan yelled after him as Rowan disappeared into the kitchen with the camera.

'All right. What do we have here?' Joan put her gloves on and kneeled beside the body. She took in every inch, before taking a thermometer out of her bag and pushing it inside the corpse's liver.

It was a rather macabre sight, but Edmonds preferred it over the maggots digging through the dead man's face.

'About eighteen degrees Celsius.' Joan read from the thermometer as she took it out and wiped the blood off it. 'Which is the same as the living room's temperature.'

'So, what's your best guess? About forty-eight hours?' Edmonds asked.

'Body temperature is the same as the surrounding temperature, maggots have appeared on his face and rigor mortis has fully set in. So, my estimate is that this man died about forty-eight hours ago.' She smiled. 'Very good, Edmonds.'

Rowan had finished photographing the kitchen and came back into the living room.

'Any wiser yet, doc?' Rowan asked against better judgement.

'If there's something you need to know, I will let you know,' Joan replied, without looking away from the bullet wound.

She lifted the body's head. 'You see that here?' she asked Edmonds, who leaned in closer.

'There's an exit wound, so we need to find a bullet somewhere.'

'Precisely. And if you compare the diameter of the wound in his forehead to the wound in the back of his head, it gives you an indication of which gun might have been used. Which would have been a…?'

Rowan looked at Edmonds closely inspecting the entry and exit wound. He didn't care much about forensics, but Joan teaching Edmonds made him jealous.

'The exit wound is only slightly larger than the entry wound,' Edmonds thought aloud. 'And the entry wound is about the same diameter as my little finger. So…' She paused for a moment. She did not want to look like a fool, especially not in front of Joan. 'My guess is a 9mm.' Edmonds gave Joan a questioning look.

'Very likely,' Joan said with a smile. 'I'll be able to give you more information after the autopsy.' Joan got up and spoke more loudly. 'Or perhaps if the gentlemen can find the bullet, the forensic lab will be able to make an exact determination.'

Edmonds smiled and got up. 'Have you photographed the upstairs yet?' she asked Rowan.

'Just about to.'

Rowan wanted to give her a snarky comment but decided against it. He didn't like anyone telling him what to do, especially if it was someone with less experience than him. Edmonds smiled at him, clearly enjoying the power she had over him in the moment.

'What took you so long?' Joan asked Brian impatiently, who led the forensic team inside. He didn't reply and took the body bag off the gurney as Edmonds walked towards the forensic experts, greeting both of them warmly.

'All right. We got one body. Joan has finished her preliminary examination and she's taking the body to the morgue now. We are still looking for a bullet, most likely a 9mm. We've taken photographs of the downstairs area. Rowan is photographing the upstairs now.'

Katrina nodded. 'We'll start with fingerprints around this area,' she said, as she pointed at the table. 'And then continue through the kitchen and bathroom and then the upstairs area. After you guys leave, we will tear up the place. Who do I call if I find anything urgent? Curtis?'

'You can call me,' Edmonds said. 'Curtis is in a meeting.'

'You got it,' Katrina replied and gestured for her colleague to start working on the table.

CHAPTER 25

For the sake of love, I ask you to stay away from me.
Before I break you, how they broke me.

'I hate it when you tell me to love you less.' As usual, she stood by the window, watching the ordinary lives of others. 'Because of all the people I know, you are in most need of love.'

The words hit him like a piece of his artwork had hit others. He could die for her words instantly, but not without a fight. His whole life he had wanted someone to speak those exact words. Never had he stopped searching for someone who wouldn't be pushed away by him. God knew he had tried, and succeeded. Everyone he had once felt a connection to, he had managed to eliminate from his life at some point.

Looking back, it had been his fault, each time again. And each time, he had regretted it. There had been some great people in his life, some of which he may have even loved. But the need to be different and independent had won his inner battle. The battle he had fought with himself over the course of many years, a battle to which there was still no end.

None of the people in his life had captured him quite like she had. He glanced over. The white sweater and light blue jeans fitted her nicely. He could see the reflection of her beautiful face in the window. Outside, the world had started to wake up, it was going to be a cloudy day.

She was dangerous, because unlike the others, she could actually see him. Not just as the man he presented himself to be, but as the man he had hidden away from the world for many years. She knew him, his guards had not even tried to defend themselves against her.

What had she done to him? And why had she chosen him, out of all the people? Those were the questions playing through his mind day and night. At times, it was those questions which kept him awake throughout the night as he watched her sleep peacefully next to him.

She was much younger, and more beautiful — in heart, soul and body. He couldn't comprehend why someone like her would choose to be with someone so broken as him. Truth was, he had become addicted to being broken. He always pretended to want an easy-going life. But he knew, she knew, he was lying.

She was the smallest chance he had at a peaceful life. So, naturally, he had pushed her away. Many times had he tried to convince her she was better off without him, hoping deep down she wouldn't ever leave him. Too many good people had obeyed his request, his begging to leave him and his convincing them that they were better off without his troubles. He needed someone to stick with him so badly, to give him more love and care. She did that, he wanted her gone.

'I'm just saying it, because you know I can't offer you anything. I don't want to hurt you.'

She didn't even bother turning around to face him, having heard that same line from him over and over again. 'You're saying it out of the goodness of your heart, are you?' She spoke without any emotion, knowing what was coming.

'Well, yes.' He spoke convincingly, almost believing it himself. 'The situation is too difficult. You know that as well. I can't guarantee you a future, can't give you what you need.' He paused, searching for something he could add to make it not sound so repetitive. 'I really care for you; I just want you to be happy.' That he had said often as well, but at least that part was genuine.

Deep down, he wanted to go up to her and take her into his arms. To tell her he loved her and to ask her never to leave his side again. He felt like a little boy next to her. She was someone he could collapse in front of, knowing she would be there to pick up the pieces.

But he didn't want to strain her with his troubles. There was so much darkness inside him. And there was darkness inside her, too, she had told him and showed him. He'd been angry. Not necessarily at her, but at the world for hurting someone so beautiful.

His scars and darkness were his to deal with. Although he couldn't handle dealing with it alone. The battle within started again. There was a healthy way and a destructive way. Everything inside him knew to tell her the truth, but he knew he couldn't. It was because he loved her so much, he wanted to protect her, from him.

Before he could speak, she turned around. Her face looked serious, unlike it ever had before. She was about to break his heart.

'Why don't you ask me how it makes me feel when you ask me to love you less?'

The repetitive discussions had driven her mad. She knew he loved her deeply. He didn't want her to leave, but he had said it so many times, it had gotten to a point where she almost believed him.

The question caught him off-guard. He wanted to run away, as far away as he could possibly get. Hoping when he'd return, she'd still be there. The chance of her leaving him scared him greatly. It made him angry, although he didn't intend it that way.

'Forget about it.'

He smiled at her warmly, hoping she would, but knowing she wouldn't.

'It makes me feel like an annoying person. I show up, with nothing to give you but love, and then you tell me you don't want it. I know you do want it, you're in desperate need of it.'

She came closer, his intention to cut the conversation short had pissed her off.

Walking away from her would give him what he wanted, temporarily. But she wouldn't allow him to get away with it that easily.

'Do you really think you're that broken? Because, frankly, I don't see it. I see it as a façade you use to keep everyone at arm's length — your way of not letting anyone in, pretending you're doing it because you care for me. We both know you're lying, so why don't you stop and let me love you?'

She spoke those words louder, hoping it would get through to him. Standing close to him, she looked deeply into his eyes, hoping he'd see the hurt he had caused.

'I won't leave you because of your darkness or troubles. I won't leave you because you want me to love you less. The only reason I'd leave you is if I felt like I was annoying you. My love is not to be considered annoying. I've been broken, brutally broken, but I can still love. And I know you can, too. Don't ever make me feel like I am annoying you, because it hurts. You don't want to hurt me, right?'

He hoped it was a rhetorical question, but to his dismay he noticed she waited for his answer. If only he could ignore her, this part of her, the part where she could see right through him. It annoyed him.

Annoyed may not be the right word, he definitely did not intend it in the way she had. She wasn't annoying him, but he wanted to push her away before she could see too much of the real him. But each time she pushed further in the opposite direction, demanding to know more of him.

Her patience had always been something he loved about her. Never did she push him to do anything he couldn't in the moment. Never had she made any requests in moments he couldn't even uphold his own standards. Even when he had broken promises, or delayed promises, she hadn't complained. Because she understood where he was coming from. He'd explain to her why he needed more time and peace, but he also knew he didn't have to explain it to her. She understood without him speaking.

Nevertheless, he'd explain it, because he wouldn't want it to be held against him at some point. There was always a chance their relationship could turn sour, although he couldn't imagine it, having felt her kind heart beat. He trusted her completely, but he also knew life sometimes forced people to make insane decisions and take life-changing stands.

Sometimes people would get cornered, they'd feel like they had nowhere left to move. She had been in those positions in her life, and he knew she could get nasty. God knew he had been in those places and he had gotten real nasty; aggressive, criminal. There was a part of him he needed to keep secret, to protect. Not from her, but from what life could do to them.

Judging by the way she looked at him, he couldn't imagine they would ever do anything to hurt each other. He felt like opening up his heart to her and tell her everything that kept him up at night and to ask her all the questions playing through his mind. Only this time, he'd really want to listen to her response, and more importantly, believe her response.

'I don't want to hurt, that is why I say what I say. You are better off…'

She interrupted him. 'Then let me love you, in the purest way I know how. It'll heal your wounds.'

Again, there was so much love he didn't deserve. It almost broke his heart to see someone fall for him the way she had. If he ever stopped caring for her, it would destroy every piece of her. Or so he thought.

'I know what you're thinking, but you have got to stop believing that. My light won't turn to darkness if you decided to move on. I care for you and I want you to be happy. But I am not stupid. I won't be broken if you move on from my love. I can see our future is difficult.'

'You must understand I don't see it that way. I look at a beautiful woman, thinking she can save me somehow. When the truth is, I don't need your saving. I'm not some project or puzzle you need to accomplish. I'm fine with you liking me, maybe even loving me, but don't centre your life around me.'

The words sounded harder than he intended them. As soon as he had finished his sentence, he immediately regretted speaking those words. They were hurtful words, ones she didn't deserve. He knew she meant well, but there was a certain truth to what he had said.

The thought of her hurting because of him made him want to leave her alone.

An expression of pain flashed over her face. The words had cut her like the knife she once used to relieve pain.

'That's quite an arrogant statement to make, don't you think? Do you honestly believe I have got no life outside of you? I truly hope you're just saying that out of spite. Spite for showing you love. Maybe you are broken… I've got many goals, all of which I had before I met you and all of which I continue to work on now that I know you. My life, love or happiness does not live or die with you. I can live without you. I just don't want to. You deserve my love. I want to give it to you, like a present. All I ask of you, is to treat it with respect.

'That is my love. It makes me happy to see you happy, but I don't love me because you love me. I love me, because I chose it to be that way. If I were to see you happy with someone else or somewhere else, then I'd be truly happy for you. You won't lose my love telling me the truth. You'll lose my love making me believe I am annoying.

'Because it took a lot of recovering and pain to still be able to love after everything that was done to me, and I will protect that piece of my soul, against anyone. I'll give it to people who need it, like you, but I won't let anyone disrespect it. My love is not annoying. Don't tell me ever again to love you less.'

She placed her warm hand against his cheek.

After all the pushing he had done, she was still here. For the first time, someone had truly shattered his walls. Every single one of them.

CHAPTER 26

Fix my eyes,
so my heart can hear the truth.

'How many were you able to identify?'

The words sounded even colder in the eerie environment.

Interpol's team of medical examiners had laid out the bodies throughout the big white space. There hadn't been enough spaces in the coolers, so they had lowered the temperature in the common area to preserve what was left of the blown-apart bodies.

Joan stood in the middle of the room, writing down a few of her last notes. She clicked the pen and stuck it into her lab coat, then sighed deeply, before finally delivering the answer no one wanted to hear.

'As far as we can see, as of now, nineteen.'

Joan had been around, she was trained to deal with these amounts of bodies and the disfigurements, as if they were jigsaw puzzles. She was good at it and loved her job, at times the idea of how macabre others found it would slip her mind. But she had a soft spot for Edmonds. Her own daughter was about her age, and she wouldn't dream of letting her near any of the horrible sights the Interpol team chose to see each day.

Edmonds nodded quietly, purposely looking away from Joan. She didn't want to appear weak and she knew it'd be hard for her to hide her emotions with Joan looking at her the way she did. It was meant sympathetically, but at this stage, it was disconcerting. There was no time for emotions, although she felt the need to collapse and cry her eyes out.

'Did you sleep at all?'

'Few hours. You?'

'Few hours.' Joan offered a smile. 'We worked in shifts through the night, taking turns sleeping in the bunk bed in my office.'

'Nineteen identified out of forty-seven…'

'Indeed.' Joan scraped her throat, stuck her hands in her pockets and started giving Edmonds the information she'd come for. 'First thing we had to do was match all limbs and other body parts blown apart in the explosion to the torsos. We managed to do most of that so far. That's how we've managed to give you the number forty-seven.'

Edmonds nodded, looking around the room in horror. Piecing bodies together seemed so surreal. Especially in the way her friend described it. She realised Joan was looking at her again and knew it was time to snap out of the emotion.

'How did you manage to identify them?'

'Mostly from pictures provided by family members who came in, wishing their loved ones weren't lying on my tables. When we had a possible match, we had them come into the morgue and take a look at the body.'

'How many males, females and children? And did you find anything significant that might help us to trace the bomber?'

'Twelve children, eight girls and four boys. Then there were twenty-one males and fourteen females. One family lost both their children…'

Edmonds didn't expect an emotional remark from her always professional friend. It soothed her knowing even the experienced medical examiner wasn't resistant to crimes like this. She wanted to offer he some sort of comfort, but before she had a chance to show any kind of empathy, Joan continued her breakdown of results.

'We've kept the pieces of bomb fragments separate and sent them to the lab. I'm sure we'll find more pieces of shrapnel, so we'll continue to collect them. The bodies most unrecognisable, were, as you'd expect, standing closest to the bomb. As we continue our autopsies, I might be able to give forensics a hand in furthering the sketch showing who was standing where. But it'll be very basic, and it'll take us time to give you more details. Besides, I'm not sure it will be of much help to your investigation.'

'I understand.'

She hadn't expected much more from the ME team. Not because they weren't qualified, but because it was a slow process. Identifying the bodies and retrieving any pieces of the bomb were really all Joan could do at this stage. After that, she'd be the one to try and offer some closure to the families and friends staying behind.

She'd have many conversations where she'd have to try and convince the broken families to not take a last look at their loved ones. To remember them as they were, not in the horrible state they were taken.

Some would respond angrily, whereas others would sob uncontrollably, and then there were those who would remain quiet throughout Joan's explanations. The shock wouldn't allow them to feel any kind of emotion. They'd just sit there and listen.

Those conversations were easiest to have, because she could remain clinical and professional in a way to detach from the horrifying reality.

The grieving process was a silly thing. Some felt the pain immediately, where others remained in this in-between world where reality hadn't set in yet. Denial, the first stage. The longer it took, the more horrifying the results, Joan often feared.

Hiding emotions and burying them had never been her way of dealing with things. Except when she was at work, that's where she always acted professional and unemotional. She had no choice, families relied on her keeping it together. But when she'd come home, or sometimes even as soon as she got into her car, she'd bawl her eyes out. Completely and utterly destroyed. That's how she'd feel for about an hour or so. After that, she'd pick herself up again and rely on her family to understand her red eyes. Thankfully, they always did.

The last member of Joan's team left the room, pushing a gurney into the hallway. The two women were left standing in the middle of the madness. There was a contrast between the two. One in a white lab coat, mid-forties and experienced in her job. The other wore a leather jacket with tight jeans and was in her mid-twenties, just starting out in the world.

The silence became unbearable and forced Edmonds to speak.

'Forty-seven… All these people had lives, dreams and fears. And now… they're just gone…'

'Yeah… Makes you wonder, doesn't it?'

CHAPTER 27

Sweet stranger,

I'm done lying. Done hiding.

I've hidden my true self for too long and I've seen what it can do to a person. If anything, it was and still is, my biggest motivation to speak up.

My Dad always hid his true self, always wore a mask. And now, looking back, I can finally name what exactly bothered me the most about our relationship; all I ever wanted was for him to be himself, to take off his mask.

It's something I hadn't previously been able to quite pinpoint. But his passing made me realise it was just that which saddened me most. I so badly wanted to know the man behind the mask. The person who was truly my father. I think I would have learned a lot from him and his struggles.

He is my example, an example of how I do not want to end up. There's so much he could have done with his life, if only he had opened up and been honest with himself.

It's so hard for me to do just that. My family knows me as the person I portray to be. They like that person and they have no idea just how far gone I was or how much of my emotions and aspirations I have been hiding.

I couldn't hurt them with my hurt. But I am also terrified for the moment when the burden outweighs the guilt.

I know I have always been looking for someone with whom I could be a hundred percent open and honest. And I've always sought that sort of a relationship outside of my family, in the atmosphere of friendship or romance.

Within those relationships I always expected to be able to drop bombshells at random moments and not have to deal with the emotions it may cause for the other party.

I never realised I was never honest with myself to begin with and I always judged the other party for not accepting my madness, inevitably leading to broken relationships and easy goodbyes.

I wish to fall in love with life again, but I know it requires a hundred percent honesty on my part to those I hold dearest to my heart.

I miss you, stranger,
wishing you were here, with love from afar.

Chapter 28

Our Father in heaven, hallowed be Your name.
Your kingdom come, Your will be done, on earth as it is in
heaven.
Give us this day our daily bread, and forgive us our debts as
we forgive our debtors.
Do not lead us into temptation,
But deliver us from the evil one.
For Yours is the kingdom, and the power and the glory forever.
Amen.

'Hello there God, it's been a while since we talked, and a lot has passed my mind since. I must say I have been looking forward to speaking with You again. You always give me some sort of sign and guidance and I think in this very moment I need just that.

'I am starting to see the same symptoms my dad carried. It scares me, because I don't want to be like him. He was a very troubled man, and my chance of ending up just like him scares me more than anything else in this world. The idea of my family and friends resenting me the way I resented him makes me want to run away from reality. But I know that is exactly what

he did, and if I did that it would be the exact same mistake he made.

'I don't want to be paranoid like him. I don't want to be hiding behind a mask like him. I don't want to fear showing the world the real me. I don't want to be anything like his disease.

'Deep down, I know this is my truth, and as a result I am completely lost. I feel as if there's three people living inside my head. One is out to destroy me, one is out to love everything and make the most of life and the third — the one in the middle — is the grounded one. This person lives in the centre of my head and isn't strong enough to beat the other two. The one who's out to destroy me lives on the left side, the ecstatic one lives on the right. I'm not sure why that matters, but that's how I perceive it to be in this moment. Although sometimes I think they're crossing over just to mess with me and make me confused.

'Do You think this is my truth? Do You believe the same I do? And if so, what should I do? I wish for it not to be true just as much as I wish for it to be true. I do not want to be sick, do not want to end up like my dad. But not having this disease would mean not having a cure or a way of dealing with how I feel. Either way, it's not really a pleasant outcome. I need Your strength to see me through this. I believe at this stage I am capable of handling everything myself, but I can feel the darkness creeping in again. I know soon enough there'll

be a craving for the poisons again, and that's when I will need Your support.

'I wish I had the guts to tell my family, to go see them or be with them. But everything is different now and I don't think they want anything to do with me any more.

'I think if I don't get help at some point, I will slip away again. I tell myself it'll be easier to resist the poisons now that I have an idea of what's wrong with me, but it's also a possibility it'll become less and less bearable as the disease progresses. That's how I see it anyway, as a progressive disease. I'm not even sure if that's how it works, but it is how I feel these personas toying with me.

'I also wish to tell you all the things I feel so very grateful for. One of which is my health. Even though I think my mental health might be in jeopardy, I know I am so lucky to be able to exercise and to be mobile. If I didn't have that in this very moment… I'm not sure what I would be doing. I imagine it though, sometimes. Right now, I consider myself to be in quite a healthy space and I cannot imagine reaching that low again where I need to fight to keep myself away from me. This one persona will come out again at some point, regardless of the groundwork I lay now, and she will fight to kill me.

'If only it could be quiet around me, if only I could have peace within my mind. The kind of peace people always tell me they feel when they are around me. I do not know why or how I am capable of portraying this *inner peace to the outside world when inside my head it's a jungle of constant battles, mixed with voices and screams. Perhaps it's just because I feel so unlike myself that I do not want anyone to see it, sense it or experience it for themselves. Perhaps I portray this peace to the outside world because I know just how much in need some of the people out there are.*

'I often wonder if society has become more negligent and selfish, or if I am purposely destroying myself by looking after other people's needs ahead of my own. I desire to live my life in a loving way. I want to know I am helping people.

'I'm scared.'

In the name of the Father,
The Son,
And the Holy Spirit.
Amen.

CHAPTER 29

'You want me to revise my statement?'

'I want you to tell the truth, as I have just told it to you.'

Jack Binckle chuckled sarcastically. It was late, and he had already been drinking. He had received several e-mails from media channels, all offering him on-air time. He rubbed his forehead. He knew that what they had offered him wasn't so much an offer as it was a demand.

'Why would I give you a way out?'

'I'm afraid you're mistaken; I am giving you one. You lied to the United Kingdom's citizens. I am here giving you viable information no other reporter has come across just yet. It's an opportunity to cleanse your name.'

'I don't need a way out.'

'Sure you do.' Director Wayne Kneebone looked around the apartment. His facial expressions showed it was far beneath his liking. 'You lost your job last year. Made a grave mistake and now you're working freelance, right?'

Jack Binckle didn't like where the conversation was headed. He felt a bribe coming, something he had been warned even before he had started working his first official job in journalism. He remembered well, his first lecture at the university. 'You will be offered bribes, especially when you are near the truth, and you will take them. Unless you hold your integrity and loyalty for our craftmanship next to your professional death.' His lecturer had been in his late fifties, early sixties. An interesting man with plenty of experience. Someone who did not need to read off the slides, someone who could just sit down on a chair behind an empty desk and tell you what you needed to know. Morale had been one of his strong suits.

'Are you telling me you will get me my job back if I revise the truth?'

'Did I say anything like that?' Kneebone turned to the person standing next to him.

Jack Binckle had recognised him as the person who had always been standing next to the Director. A complete fool and spineless persona, in Jack Binckle's opinion.

'I didn't hear you say that,' the assistant immediately replied to his boss. He looked nervous, uncomfortable even. As if he too, was under duress.

'I want you to leave now. Thank you for walking into my apartment in the middle of the night and offering me a bribe, but I will not stand for it.'

He walked over to the front door and kept it open, waiting for the two men to walk through it. To his annoyance, they did not, and stayed put. The atmosphere had become threatening.

'Mr Binckle, I understand you have no faith in the accuracy of the story which we have just laid out for you. I understand it's strange to you I would personally come and tell you of such a thing, after hours. But here's the thing, I am not *asking* you to leak this story, I am *ordering* you to do so. Your little show has put me in a tough position. I am merely asking you for some help getting out of this tough spot. Who knows, perhaps you will find yourself in a tough spot sooner or later. I would imagine you'd want a friend rather than an enemy within Interpol. Don't you think?'

CHAPTER 30

When everything was taken from me,
and they had beaten me down completely,
I kept going.
And today,
that makes me DANGEROUS.

'What made you decide to change your life?'

Vanima sighed, pulling at the seam of her blouse. She had a few reasons why she was glad she had changed her life, all of which she knew off the top of her head. But she couldn't immediately name an incident which had triggered her to change her life and to get sober.

'Was it an isolated event or did several events and emotions just keep on stacking up?'

'I was forced to stop running.' Vanima paused, carefully remembering what exactly made her change her lifestyle. 'His death changed everything. In a way… it gave me answers to questions I never really thought I had.'

The therapist nodded understandingly.

'I saw my future in his death.' She paused again, realising she had phrased it oddly. 'Or does that sound strange?'

'Not at all.' The therapist gave her an encouraging smile.

'With his passing, a lot of emotions rose to the surface within me. And I think it was the first time I was finally able to voice, to myself, the truth about what I was doing.'

'And what was that?'

'Putting other people's lives in danger with my alcohol abuse. He knew, he had tried to get me sober. But I had refused. Although no report said anything about me being under the influence that day… and no agent knows about it… I feel as if I did contribute to it. I knew right then and there, that the reality had gotten too close. So close, other people could find out if they chose to.'

'Is that when you decided you would change your life for the better?'

'No… strangely enough, it wasn't. That moment wasn't really just one moment. There was a time-span of several weeks after his death where I started envisioning myself getting sober. The day he died, I knew I needed to get sober. But it took nearly another two months for me to gain the courage to do just that.'

'You came to terms with your toxic traits and started taking responsibility?'

'That's what it boils down to. And I never realised that until he passed. It was only then that I was forced to see it. I finally stopped making excuses.'

'Why do you keep saying "forced"? Who forced you?'

'I don't know. It wasn't as much a person, I think, as much as it was life.' She paused again, not wanting to sound vague, but also not having a clear answer. 'I felt really horrible for not being there when he passed. I mean, I could have gone back, could have been there for him in his final moments. But I didn't. If I had, I would have gotten caught, and that would have been, at the very least, the end of my career. I hated myself for thinking that way.'

'That's when the self-harm got worse?'

'Yeah… I needed to punish myself for being so cold-hearted. Because even after he had passed I was selfish, thinking about how it affected me and not him. I *hate* myself.' She spoke the words with determination, as if she needed to convince the therapist she was right to hate herself.

Hoping for a response, she stayed quiet for some time, but the therapist didn't say anything to deny or confirm her statement. The silence pushed Vanima to continue, to figure out on her own, that her statement was ridiculous.

'I just couldn't… couldn't bear the thought of seeing him like that. But I also couldn't collapse afterwards, because it would cost me my job.'

Emotions welled up behind her eyes.

'And so, you hid physically and emotionally in a foreign country. But when you needed to return, you kept away emotionally and hid your physical scars.'

It wasn't a question, but Vanima nodded in agreement. 'I was empty. I had nothing left to give, and the last bit of energy I did have I used to not be myself.'

'But why?'

'I couldn't hurt them with my hurt.'

'Why not, though?'

Vanima shrugged. 'Because I was guilty.'

'Do you still feel guilty?'

'Has the past changed? I wasn't there when I should have been, when he needed me.' She nearly shouted this time. 'How could they ever care for me after such a thing? I left him alone to die. Tell me how that gives me any permission to live?'

CHAPTER 31

'Raise,' Kneebone said confidently, and put a twenty pound note on the table.

The man across from him, dressed in a simple black t-shirt and jeans, scratched his beard. It was a move he made each time he wasn't sure whether he'd win or lose his hand.

Patrick, sitting beside his friend, tried his best to control his laughter. He didn't know much about poker, but he knew Kneebone's play. He was clearly bluffing, and he'd lose if the man with the beard were to call his twenty pounds, but at the same time Patrick knew the man wouldn't. Kneebone hadn't lost a single hand whenever he had raised, and he counted on the man with the beard to know that. That was Kneebone's game. Win, win, win whenever he raised, until he came to the point where everyone would fold no matter when he'd raise.

'Fold,' the man spoke, clearly annoyed with himself for not pulling through. 'What you have?' he asked in an East-European accent.

'Not telling.' Kneebone smiled, amused, collecting the notes from the centre of the table.

The man with the beard mumbled an insult under his breath in his mother tongue.

'Another game for you, gents?' the woman, dressed in a mini skirt and a deep-cut V-neck, asked with a charming smile.

'Last one for us,' Kneebone said, and nodded at Patrick, who agreed with a small nod, relieved to be going home soon.

Although he loved spending time with Kneebone, he could get a little too much to handle when he' lost. He had been on a winning streak so far, and Patrick wished for that to remain in this last hand. If not, they could be here till the early-morning hours. Patrick had often experienced that.

The woman dealt the cards with a certain flair and waited for everyone to put in their first hand.

Patrick, staring at his own hand remained with the absolute minimum call-in of ten pounds. A five of hearts and a ten of spades was not going to get him much good. The first call remained at ten pounds for everyone playing.

The woman dealt the first three cards and laid them out in the middle of the table. A seven of hearts and two aces appeared — one of hearts and one of diamonds. *Check or fold*.

They had never played for the big bucks. They couldn't possibly. Kneebone's wife would undoubtedly find out, and even though their marriage was one of convenience and status, he was not about to let her into his little secret of backroom poker. It was illegal — he was Interpol's director. The shame it would bring on him, on their marriage. No, she would never know. For Kneebone, it was the sheer brilliance of the game that kept bringing him back. The people watching, the spotting of the tells his opponents had. One would scratch his beard, others would cough, some would drink. Kneebone was a steady poker player. One of the many reasons he remained on the table with the low buy-in. He didn't want to deal with the stress of losing thousands. At most, he'd lose hundreds, enough for him to know when to stop. Although, he hardly ever did. He kept coming back for more, or less. That's why he'd bring Patrick along. He knew when to stop.

Patrick was third in line to say 'check' and resisted the urge to look at Kneebone, quietly awaiting his move.

'Raise,' Kneebone spoke and put a five pound note in front of him.

The table had started to wear off, the green mat which had once been bright and clean had now become brown and ripped on the sides.

The man with the beard was next in line and put his cards down. 'Fold.'

The two remaining men followed his lead. Only Patrick was left to decide whether to raise or fold. Naturally, he chose to fold. He didn't have the right cards, but he also wouldn't dream of beating Kneebone at poker. He had just finished his fourth glass of whiskey.

'Thank you for tonight. See you again next time.' Kneebone, feeling fulfilled, stuck the notes in his wallet and put on his long, brown winter coat. 'You ready?' he asked Patrick, who stood up willingly.

'Thanks, guys.' Patrick tipped the woman her regular twenty pound tip and followed Kneebone out the door.

Outside, the street was wet, but it wasn't raining any more. The sky was dark and cloudy, a streetlight tried showing some light into the dark alley. Above Kneebone's head, rose a cloud of cigarette smoke.

'Started again, yes?' Patrick asked, lighting himself a cigarette, too.

'Might as well,' Kneebone replied, feeling tipsy. 'Had fun?'

'As usual.' The taste of nicotine filled his lungs. He tied the buttons of his coat. He wasn't really cold, but the dark, cloudy sky always made him feel a little uneasy. It had made him wish he was lying in bed, curled up underneath a warm blanket. Whether he was sober, tipsy, drunk or invincible, the dark sky would always have that effect on him.

'Here's what I'm thinking,' Kneebone started, not standing very steady on his feet any more. He could normally handle his liquor pretty well, but he hadn't eaten all day and the stress had gotten to him. Four whiskeys and cigarettes on an empty stomach, he'd regret that in the morning. 'We should kill Jack Binckle.'

Patrick did not move, did not speak. Waiting for his boss to say, 'Just kidding'. But it didn't come. The sentence lingered in the air as if it was a death sentence on its own.

'You're kidding, right?' he finally asked, and watched Kneebone turn around, now facing him.

Kneebone took another puff from his cigarette and inhaled deeply.

'No.'

'What…? You can't possibly be serious?' Patrick started walking slowly towards Kneebone, who was standing a few metres away from him, underneath the yellow streetlight.

'Tell me why not? For years I have worked to get Interpol to where it is today. And then some… some self-righteous piece of *shit* comes in and starts yapping. We serve a higher purpose!'

Patrick realised that Kneebone would not back down. There was a certain determination in his eyes that scared him.

'It's just the liquor talking. Come on, let's get you home.'

'It's not the liquor talking! The liquor is just merely giving me the courage to speak my mind for once! Look at you… Throughout your whole career you've been at my beck and call. No career of your own. If I go down, so will you. Don't you get that?'

The words hit Patrick like a bullet. Not because Kneebone was being rude, but because he was right.

There had been an unspoken relation between the two of them, one where Patrick was always the one to clean up the mess Kneebone needed help with. And for what? Years had gone by where Patrick had been the loyal employee every employer sought after. And in return he got a nice salary, a car, and he was invited to high-class events. But he had always remained the sidekick. He hadn't minded it, he cared for Kneebone.

'Oh, don't give me that face. You know it's true. You've dedicated your whole life to the Service, and you didn't even get to wear a badge. What are you going to do after this? Get an assistant job for some ludicrously low pay rate with some asshole boss? You and I.' He placed his both hands on Patrick's shoulders. 'We're in this together. We are a union, you and me.'

Patrick turned his face away from Kneebone's face, his breath reeked of a combination of hunger, cigarettes and heavy liquor.

'Wayne… you're drunk,' he tried again. 'I need to get you home.'

'Ha!' Kneebone spun around on his heels and almost fell over, quickly holding on to the garbage bin. 'Do you even hear yourself? *You* need to get *me* home? I'm not your wife! You don't need to 'get me home'. I can take care of myself, Patrick. What I need from you, is for you to understand that this Jack Binckle, is in the way of our careers and retirement. Because, like I said, if I go, you go. They won't keep you, there'd be too many questions hanging over your head. The media will chase you down, bribe you to do interviews. You won't cave, I know that. But let's spare ourselves the misery and put an end to this.'

It had become painfully obvious to Patrick that Kneebone was not kidding. He was drunk, yes. But he had been drunker and acted more rationally.

'Wayne… that's an insane plan… We can't 'end' Jack Binckle. There'll be questions.' Patrick tried playing into Kneebone's fantasy with rational thoughts.

'Not as many as they're asking us now.'

He lit another cigarette and looked at Patrick, who had now impatiently started pacing back and forth around the dark, wet alley.

'Good.'

Patrick stood still. 'Good?'

'Yeah.' He took a puff from his cigarette and tried blowing the smoke out of his mouth in circles. He failed miserably and started coughing.

'Good. When you pace, it means you're thinking. At least you're considering my offer.'

'*Your offer*,' Patrick repeated cynically. 'An offer I can't refuse?' he added, even more cynically.

'Yes! Exactly!' Kneebone used his hands to give extra power to his words, the cigarette loosely hanging from his lips. A smile shaped itself as he stared into space.

The sight frightened Patrick. It was as if his friend Wayne had left and another person had replaced him. A cry of laughter startled him and made him walk out of the alley, their hiding place. It was just two women, both obviously drunk. He turned around and walked back to Kneebone, who was still staring into space. Patrick placed his hand on his friend's shoulder.

'Wayne, come on. Let's go home. This is no place to talk about these kinds of things.'

Kneebone looked at his friend. For a moment he had no idea where he was, and he looked around in confusion.

'Okay, but let's go to your house. My place is no good to discuss these things, either. The missus...' He pointed at his wedding ring and made a face of annoyance.

Patrick sighed and agreed, glad to get out of a dark alley and into an atmosphere of privacy. 'Let's get to your driver.'

For special occasions like this, Kneebone relied on his discreet driver, who had worked for him for many years. There were some occasions, very much like this one, that simply couldn't go through Interpol's drivers or a public taxi service. Kneebone's public status, especially in these days, could easily be used to blackmail him. If there were to be a picture of the two of them together in a dark alley at an alleged illegal poker game, their careers would be over before the sun came up.

Throughout the ride home, nothing was said. Even Kneebone, with his inebriated mind, seemed to realise talking about a potential hit on a journalist in the presence of an albeit discreet driver was not the best idea.

Words of common courtesy were exchanged between Patrick and the driver as Kneebone wandered off towards Patrick's front door. The house, built just after World War II, was identical to its neighbours, and far above Patrick's pay grade.

A few years ago, after the death of his father, an inheritance had allowed him to purchase the property. Of course, Kneebone, too, had had a hand in it.

Patrick swiftly pushed Kneebone away from the door knocker and told him to be quiet. There was no need to have the neighbours wake up and look at Interpol's director banging loudly on a door with another male, in the middle of the night, clearly drunk. The stories that would create.

The home, too large for Patrick himself, was kept in a clean and tidy way. As one would expect from a bachelor, who worked full-time organising another man's life, there were very little personal objects in the living room. There were some pictures of places he had travelled to and some books, neatly stacked, but that was about it. The black leather couch and the wooden floor showed no sign of having had much company.

Kneebone had thrown his coat onto a designer chair and stared at one of the pictures on the wall.

'I didn't know you went to Egypt.' He pointed at a photo with pyramids on it.

Patrick sighed, clearly tired of having to deal with the drunk version of his friend. 'Yes, you do know. But perhaps you don't remember in this state.'

He walked over to the liquor cart and picked an expensive whiskey. *Might as well.* He poured a double for himself, and a regular for his friend.

The couch made that leathery noise as the men took their place and sipped their whiskey. A few minutes were spent in silence; Patrick contemplating whether he should revisit the earlier subject, Kneebone contemplating a plan.

Eventually, it was Patrick who spoke and expressed his dislike of Kneebone's earlier comments. Although Kneebone remained silent throughout his entire plea, and appeared to be listening, the first words out of Kneebone's mouth sounded scarier than those he had spoken before. It was only then that Patrick realised his friend was deadly serious and it wasn't just the liquor talking any more.

Again, Patrick tried pleading with him, and again Kneebone didn't budge. The more sense he tried talking into Kneebone, the more it fuelled his friend to contemplate a real plan. Another silence fell and Patrick went for a refill.

'I know how to do it. A hitman.'

'A hitman?' Patrick kept his eyes focussed at the bottom of his drink. Scared to look at the stranger sitting next to him.

'Yes. He has lost his wife recently, and his job. He's a wannabe journalist digging for dirt on innocent men doing their job.' The last sip of liquor slid down his throat. 'We can make up some background story.'

'We?'

An ice-cold feeling took possession of his body and made his heart drop to the floor.

****

Jack Binckle sat in front of his computer. His cursor kept on flicking and disappearing. If he stared at it long enough, it almost got him into some sort of a trance. *There it is, gone again.* A loud bang snapped him out of it. It came from the neighbour's apartment. The lady living next door was laughing loudly and had obviously picked up male company.

This evening's conversations had been weird. They had threatened him without saying so directly, just like any great politician would. It happened daily, on the news. The government robbed its citizens of their rights with threats. Of course, that is not how the common people saw it. Some watched the news to seem intelligent, some watched the news to fall asleep. There was only a very small minority who actually saw and heard what the newsreaders said between the lines.

Everybody he had met had had an opinion about Donald Trump becoming president. Everyone had an opinion about the uprising of the Islamic State. Citizens had an opinion on refugees coming into 'their' country. But if anyone was to ask a follow-up question on their opinion, none of them had anything useful to say. Their tone of voice would turn to anger and their arguments to shit.

The laughing of his next-door neighbour died down and turned into moaning. Frustrated, Jack Binckle decided he needed a late-night walk around the town to make up his mind.

With his hands in his pockets, he walked towards the water. The sound of water always calmed him down, which was exactly what he needed right now. Having arrived, he picked a spot overlooking the Thames and watched the water flow. He unzipped his coat a little and took out the orange bottle of pills, stacked away in his inner pocket.

In the background he could hear people shouting and laughing out loudly. Everyone around him seemed to have forgotten about the drama which had occurred. They had moved on with their lives. Getting drunk, meeting up with lovers. The pressure was weighing down on him. *Which way to go?* The truth seemed to get away further and further. There was a daunting feeling on his mind which wouldn't allow him to look at the issue objectively. How could he? He was the issue. It was up to him to decide how the citizens of the UK would wake up tomorrow.

Buzzing interrupted his train of thought. Hoping it wouldn't be his ex-wife, he took the phone out of his jeans pocket. It was her. He swiped the rejection button and put the device on silent.

He knew what he had to do. Frankly, he was surprised it had taken him that long to figure it out. It was so damn clear what had to be done — his heart had told him and so had his brain. He smiled and looked up to the sky. The prospect made him feel at one with himself. It was a feeling he had missed. The feeling of simply knowing what needed to be done. He knew, he'd go against them.

CHAPTER 32

Everybody can bring good news,
only a few can deliver bad news.

'Curtis!'

Rowan and Edmonds came walking towards him in haste.

'We've got something.'

'Okay, what is it?'

The three of them walked through the busy hallway towards their office as Rowan began his briefing.

'Just before the Underground bombing, somebody made an anonymous phone call.' He handed Curtis a sheet of paper, which had the phone record, marked in red, on it.

'The person who made the call spoke with a Middle Eastern accent and discussed everything in code, which is why the police officer who answered the call didn't immediately pick up on it. He didn't mention 'bombing' or 'deaths'. Instead, he said, 'I have a Valentine's Day present for you. I will be cleaning your city, I will free you from the whores. From us for the whores.'

Curtis stopped walking abruptly and turned around, which caused Rowan to bump into him.

'The man spoke so calmly, she didn't believe him to be a threat in the first place. She thought it was just some nutjob,' Edmonds chipped in, as they stood in the chaotic common area.

'She tried asking the man for his name and more details as to what he was on about. But he did not give her any additional information. Our tracing programme wasn't able to pinpoint the location from where the man had called. I forwarded the call-log to Flynn and he told me the call was re-routed through several different countries. He's trying to pinpoint its original location now, but I don't think we'll get much out of it. And even if we do, that place will have been abandoned.'

Curtis shook his head. His mind had just flashed back, many years in time.

'Have you listened to the recording?'

'Well, yes. It was barely ten seconds.'

'Then you can confirm the sentence 'From us to the whores' had a hiccup in it?'

'Yes… how did you…?'

'And you thought it must have been his accent?'

'Yes… Why? What else is there?'

Curtis sighed, his worst fear had just become a reality. 'He must have said: 'From AkQus to the whores.' His look nearly penetrated Rowan.

'Yes, that is exactly what it sounded like,' Rowan replied, perplexed.

'What's AkQus?' Edmonds asked.

The team took a seat in their office, as Curtis remained standing, giving them the run-down of everything he knew.

'The Man. That's how they call him. Nobody knows his name or origin. Only their inner circle has had the 'honour' of meeting him in person. The Man is the leader of a terrorist organisation by the name of AkQus. They have been around twenty, maybe thirty years. But we're completely in the dark as to who their members are and how they operate.'

'I have never even heard of them,' Edmonds agreed.

'All we have to go on is myths and circumstantial evidence. It's all very secretive.'

'What do you know?' Rowan asked.

'About twenty years ago, The Man slowly started recruiting more people to join his organisation and allowed AkQus to evolve into multiple sub-divisions. But he didn't just recruit random people with a taste for crime. He recruited agents from all over the world. At some point, nearly all big intelligence agencies had at least two people within AkQus. Mossad, CIA, FBI, Interpol, SÄPO... the list went on and on.

'He started moulding these agents and infected them with his ideology. And surely, he booked success with some of them. Perhaps those agents had joined his point of view, or maybe they could, for the first time in their lives, finally speak their truth out loud.

'Cleaning up the world of dirty people, that is their motto. They refer to them as 'whores'. Not in the prostitution sense of the word, but the dirty sense of the word. Dirty meaning politicians. Politicians who changed their opinion with each favour they received. For some that may have been a bigger paycheck, for others a higher position, but for many it would come down to drugs and actual prostitutes. AkQus prides itself on not pursuing financial gain. Therefore, no paper trail or digital footprint are left behind.

'They recruited a suicide bomber, who successfully carried out their first attack at a government house in the Middle East. It killed many governmental employees, but no real politicians. Many of their attacks are not about killing politicians, but more so about pressuring politicians to come clean to the public. It's why they are not known. These attacks happen plenty and for some reason they have never claimed their attacks. In their opinion, politicians don't need to die physically, but they must die politically.'

'And now they're here,' Rowan stated.

'Yes, but what's their goal?' Edmonds wondered.

CHAPTER 33

Like a sole tree in an open field.
I suddenly realised, I was all alone.
Do you know what that's like?

'Even when you weren't near to me, I always felt your presence close to me.'

The woman peeked out the window in-between the curtain and the wall. Night had set and the village had turned dark.

It was only seven p.m., most families had finished their dinners and some neighbours were walking their dogs. The small park looked unsafe at this hour, although she knew it wasn't. The block was nice, organised and quiet. Perhaps in a parallel universe it could have been her safety harbour. But she had travelled, she had come from a different background and she knew she would have to act if she lived here.

The families surrounding the house looked so happy and peaceful, although experience had taught her all people lied and all people showed their lives to be more put together than they truly were.

A part of her wished she could do it. To find a guy who would work a nine-to-five job, someone she could marry and bicker with over unimportant things like laundry and money. Someone she'd fight with when their families wouldn't approve of each other. Someone she could fall asleep with, day after day. Their future would have a couple of kids, probably a boy and a girl. They'd grow up to be average kids who would then continue to live the same type of lifestyle their parents had built for them.

But no, deep down, she didn't really want that to be her. The stability called her name often, but her need to stand out would always win the battle. It wouldn't take long before she got bored here.

He didn't reply. His body was hunched over the table. His nose nearly pressing against the gun in his hand.

'What are you planning to do?'

She wasn't scared. From the very first moment they had met she knew something was off about him, but she had never, not even for a moment, felt unsafe in his presence. He wouldn't hurt her.

His presence had a huge impact on her. It made her vulnerable and exposed her to an unknown world. A world she never would have dreamt of entering, but now that she had gotten close to it, she had started to understand why AkQus had created that world in the first place. She wasn't involved, but she was naïve.

'Who's the gun meant for?' she pressured.

'It's for a friend.'

He finished cleaning the final part and started piecing it back together again.

'It's time for this friend to know his place. Don't worry, I won't actually use it.'

He offered her a reassuring smile, and she took it. They hadn't slept together, hadn't felt the need for it. The attraction they felt towards each other was purely one of the mind.

'Please stay away from the window. They're surely watching us. I noticed they also placed a listening device next to the kitchen door. The one that opens to the backyard.'

'They did?'

She stepped away from the window in surprise.

'Is that normal?'

'It's what they do. It's why we're in the bedroom.'

She nodded and looked at the perfectly made bed. The red spread with colourful pillows looked comfortable and her tired body ached to lay down for a bit.

CHAPTER 34

Patrick poured two cups of coffee and sat down at his kitchen table across from Kneebone, who looked surprisingly well despite the previous night's occurrences.

Quietly, Patrick hoped the subject discussed the previous night would remain in the past. The ice-cold look on Kneebone's face had haunted him in his sleep.

'Did you think about what we discussed last night?'

Cold sweat appeared on Patrick's back and he sat his cup of coffee back down. Uncomfortably, he tried scraping his throat, trying to buy himself some time to get away from replying that heinous question. 'Yes, you were an absolute idiot and I won't have any part in it,' is what he wished he had said, but his inferiority didn't allow him to say that.

So, instead, his hoarse voice spoke the words, 'What about last night?' It took everything within him to keep himself from trembling and maintaining his normal facial expressions.

'Jack Binckle.'

Kneebone spoke the words loudly and over-articulated to make a point. The look on his face and the colour in his eyes suggested everything Patrick had feared.

'Ehm… I-I-I'm not sure what to tell you on that p-particular matter.'

The attempt to show confidence had failed miserably. Nervousness made him stutter, as did other situations where he felt under pressure.

'Listen, Patrick.' Kneebone leaned forward and pushed the floral coffee cup to the side. 'I want him dead. He's trouble. You're either in or you're out.'

The words lingered in the air for a good fifteen seconds, during which Patrick was too afraid to speak. There was no choice. If he didn't do it, he'd still have the knowledge of it. There was little chance Kneebone himself would do the dirty work, and most likely he wouldn't *allow* him to do his dirty work.

In the end, the man was his boss, and despite the fact they had been a professional duo for quite some time, there were apparently still thoughts his boss hadn't shared with him. The decision to kill someone wasn't born overnight.

'All right then.' Kneebone got up, clearly unsatisfied with his silence, and began to move his way towards the other end of the room.

Patrick realised he had no choice. His boss, his friend, Interpol's director, had just told him, in confidence, that Jack Binckle would soon be dead, and it would be because of him. He had basically ordered a hit in front of him, just without telling him the exact time and location. He was in, and there was no way out. The only thing he could do now was to stay on Kneebone's good side.

'As long as I don't have to do the dirty work.'

Kneebone turned around and smiled. 'Oh, for heaven's sake, Patrick! Why would I let you do the dirty work? I just need your help to plan it all out.'

He walked back towards the table and spread his arms.

A gesture of friendship, a gesture of animosity? Regardless, Patrick got up and embraced his superior.

CHAPTER 35

The small bottle of red wine fitted nicely in her hand; she wouldn't even need a glass. There wasn't necessarily anything she needed to punish herself for, there wasn't even anything so horribly wrong she needed to escape from. The problem was, she wanted to escape. To be gone, to be out of it and to sin uncontrollably until the morning, when she'd regain control and decide to never do it again.

Slowly, she twisted the lid off the bottle. The blue label, describing the wine region and the flavour of the wine, matched the lid exactly. In her right hand, she held the unscrewed lid and her left held her sin. She kept it far away from her face so she wouldn't smell it, not yet. She wanted to both savour this moment as much as overthink it.

Millions of reasons popped into her mind, each lamer than the rest. They were no reasons, only excuses for her to justify pushing her lips against the bottle and pouring the sweet sin down into her body.

She knew what to do, what was right. But she also knew what she wanted to do. She brought the bottle closer to her face and inhaled the sweet smell of freedom, the kingdom of escape. An entire world stocked away in such a little bottle. If she really could just have an honest drink, her life would be freer.

That was the best excuse she came up with. But she also knew if she really was in a place where she could have just one drink and then walk away, there would be no need to lie to herself about it. Because, in all honesty, she didn't know why she felt the need to drink again. Her life was better than it had been in a long time, and she was proud of the lifestyle she had created for herself. It was a healthy lifestyle, for both body and soul.

Again, she inhaled the sulphites, knowing she could get drunk on the smell alone — it had been too long. Within a split second, she resisted the urge to empty the bottle at once, down her throat. Her left hand clenched around the bottle, holding it tighter than necessary. The sharp edges of the lid pressed into the skin of her right hand. She could hear herself breathing heavily. Again, she was overcome with the urge, and she clenched her hands even tighter. The breathing got heavier, and quicker.

This wasn't normal, even her sick mind knew that. Her heart beat in her throat — sheer excitement. She knew as soon as she was to take a sip, she would feel guilty for a long time. And then she would use that as a real reason to continue the drinking. This wasn't a one-time thing — this was a vicious circle.

She thought back, eyes closed, to the conversation she had had with herself in the shower. A conversation which had been about nothing, all the while just trying to find a reason to start drinking again. But in the end, she had stood there with the water pouring over her head, looking down at her naked body and pushing the razor blade against her left wrist. She hadn't cut herself, it would be too obvious, but she had considered other, less visible places to cut.

It wasn't just a drink and it wouldn't be just one time. She was still sick, but in a different way from what she had experienced before. It had been four months since her last drink. According to science it had taken ninety days for her to create the new lifestyle she had grown so fond of.

She screwed the lid back onto the bottle and placed it back down on the ground. Feeling confused, proud, guilty, but most of all: scared.

CHAPTER 36

An hour to the East in the centre of London, Jack Binckle had just ordered his second cup of coffee. The small café was buzzing with people's whispers, all detailing who knew someone who had passed away at the Westminster station and more so discussing who in their small group was the worst affected by the terrorist attack. Here and there people had started blaming the minority groups no one really knew, such as the refugees, Arabs, or if all else failed: Muslims in general.

Jack Binckle ignored all of the useless banter and instead focussed on his red laptop on the small table in front of him. The cursor kept on flicking, asking Jack Binckle to decide how far to take his truth and what to keep hidden in his head, for now.

The red laptop had been a birthday present from his ex-wife. One she had selected mainly because she liked the colour so much and because all he did was 'use Word to type stories anyway'. In her eyes, there was no reason to invest in a more advanced model with bigger memory and better security. She didn't believe his 'stories' were that important someone would hack into his computer and publish them as their own or make them disappear altogether. That was something which only happened when dealing with government documents, or in the United States.

Sometimes, he thought back to her reasoning and explanations and wondered how he had ever been able to fall in love with her. He'd consider the possibility of himself having changed, but he always came back to the same conclusion: *she* had become more superficial throughout their marriage.

He had pretended to be pleased with the present, agreeing the colour was nice and promising he would take it to work every day. At the time he couldn't stand to break her heart, looking at her eyes staring back at him filled with hope. Now, however, he wished he had told her the truth. For nearly a year and a half he had brought the much too heavy laptop to work. He had never taken it out of his bag and used the company computer instead, which had the best firewall installed on it and was heavily password-protected. It was around that time he had started showing up at night as well to use the company computers to further his work, telling his ex-wife he could only log onto the required server from the office. She had believed him.

Today he had decided to bring that laptop in a sense of melancholy. The recent events had made him miss her and he caught himself hoping she thought of him, too. However, he was still reluctant to take her calls, knowing she only called to try and get him to stop what he was doing. The cursor was still flicking, patiently waiting until he would finally make up his mind.

The woman in the hospital bed crossed his mind again. He had thought of her a lot. All other victims from the bombing didn't have a face. The only place he had seen them was on pictures where they had been happy and living their lives. Usually, they were smiling in those photos, the families wanted to remember them that way, as happy individuals. They purposely wanted to push away the thought of them ever having cried or felt pain. Their last moments on the face of the earth would not be thought of for a long time, not until somewhere in the final stage of mourning, when their mind finally allowed them to go to that place. But for now, they were happy individuals smiling into the camera at some party, event or family gathering. Not knowing that same picture would be used a certain period of time later at the Underground's memorial site.

The girl in the hospital bed had a different face. Her face was burned onto his cornea and he simply couldn't shake the thought of having wronged her by taking the picture. He knew it would be wrong to publish it, but he also knew it would be a great cash-in. Something in his gut told him not to publish anything about the girl; no story, no picture. He couldn't quite grasp the reasoning behind it, as usually goes with gut feelings; a rational explanation is nowhere to be found.

Jack Binckle tried to separate his emotions from his professional view, hoping to gain perspective on why his gut told him not to publish. He had always followed his instinct and it had never failed him, but he worried his emotions and the depression interfered with his instinct.

The girl had a real face along with a broken body. There was an in-between stage for her; the one where she hadn't died yet and was forced to deal with what had happened to the best of her ability, or the machine's ability, if she wanted to survive.

That remained his biggest concern; whether she had the will or intent to survive.

He opened the zip file, which contained the pictures. Even with her eyes closed and attached to all the medical equipment, it seemed like she wouldn't be one to mess with. There was something about the young woman which made Jack Binckle think he had seen her somewhere before, but he could not quite place it. or perhaps her features had ot so well-known to him, as her stared at her every day. He copied and pasted one of the close-ups and cut the edges away until all that was left was her face.

Her brown bangs slightly covered her forehead. She had strong features, yet feminine. She had beauty, but not the average kind the crowd would condemn as 'pretty'. He uploaded her cropped photograph into his facial-recognition software. It was a silly little program, rather amateurish, but he still felt as if it would help him in some way. The software only gave him access to publicly known platforms, such as social media or easily hacked security cameras from around public areas. The software was illegal and he rarely used it, but using it to identify his Jane Doe made him feel more of a reporter.

The program started running and he allowed it to do its job as he re-opened his Word document, where his cursor was still patiently waiting for him to make a move. He looked around the café, hoping to find the answer written on the walls.

Not finding a thing there, he decided to go with his gut and not mention the girl's survival for the time being. Just as he started typing, he heard a small ding. His program had found a ninety-two percent match on a public platform outside of the United Kingdom.

CHAPTER 37

I think people don't abandon a sinking ship unless they see a rescue boat. But I also think your boat isn't out at sea, it's in the harbour. Perhaps you should ask yourself why that is. Because I believe you, out of all people, deserve someone who will sail the rough waters with you.

As she lay there, the silence struck her. It was three a.m., the television was on mute and the neighbours were sleeping. Outside, there wasn't a single noise; no cars, no barking dogs, not even a sound of wind or rain. Nothing. Absolute silence.

Thoughts ran through her head, all dying out within seconds. There was no need to masturbate again. She questioned whether she could make the peace last longer by cutting, but that thought disappeared, too. The urge to drink made absolutely no sense. Loud music in her ears wouldn't give her this kind of peace, either. The need to run seemed useless. Food didn't even cross her mind.

That was it. All her temptations — orgasms, drinking, cutting, loud music and running — didn't exist any more in that moment. There was utter peace and quiet around her. In any other moment, it would have driven her nuts, to the brink of one of her temptations. But this time, it was different. She could lay there for hours, like she was dead.

She slightly opened her mouth and stared at a small brown dot in the ceiling, pretending to be a corpse. Perhaps it was macabre to some, but to yoga instructors it was a form of exercise, and to her, it meant peace.

The brown dot didn't move, didn't change shape, didn't turn into some rollercoaster of thoughts and emotions. It simply remained a small, brown dot on the ceiling.

If death was an option right there, in that very moment, without having to lift a single finger, she would have chosen it. Being a corpse was the best thing to life. A corpse was dead and therefore had no thoughts.

In that moment, her mind had gone completely silent. She'd ticked off her list of temptations and felt no desire to pursue any one of them. Knowing that feeling wouldn't last long, she continued to stare at the brown dot. If it had a brain, it would probably still be unaware as to how much of a difference its mere being presented to her.

The only thing keeping her from wanting to disappear permanently in that moment was the fact she lay naked. It wouldn't be a pretty sight for whomever was to find her. Then again, if she was dead, that would be no longer be her problem.

Silence in her head. If that's what the ordinary people experienced each day, she could understand their happiness. It was a pleasant place to be.

A message from him broke her inner peace.

Meet me at the terrace.

She read the message, without opening it, and stuffed her phone under her pillow.

She pushed her body in the upright position again and leaned against a stack of pillows, arranged in such a way to have kept her sitting up straight. Another cigarette showed off its toxicity in the shape of relaxing smoke. She wasn't nervous any more; he had unknowingly taken care of that. This would be the beginning of the end, an ending she'd craved for what seemed an eternity.

Meet me at the terrace.

Inevitably, her curiosity won, needing to know what it was he wanted from her after his discovery. Perhaps he hadn't even realised, and he just wanted some alone-time with her, leading to excitement and then regret or annoyance.

As she walked down the stairs, she found herself in a battle between what she wanted him to say or do. Partially, she wished he'd sit her down and tell her how special, important and irreplaceable she was.

Her watch had stayed behind in her room, he knew anyway. She found her way through the dark house and stood still in the kitchen. The door to the terrace was closed and the kitchen tiles felt cold. She felt naked without her watch, exposed. It wasn't for the fact she was wearing a tight white t-shirt without a bra. The scars were visible, she was visible.

Momentarily, she pondered the thought of going back upstairs, he hadn't seen her yet. She could still go back and put her watch on, maybe put some socks on, too. If he really hadn't understood what those cuts on her wrist meant, she may be on the verge of stupidly showing off a side of herself she wanted to hide. A side especially he shouldn't know about.

Too late, he had gotten out of his seat, and spotted her bright white t-shirt. If it hadn't been a full moon, she may have gotten away with it. Slowly, she opened the door and stepped out of the air-conditioned room into a warm sea breeze. Although it was night-time, the temperature still allowed for them to be out without a jumper. The northern wind, blowing in from the warmer areas near the equator, made the setting perfect for two lovers sneaking around. Her dark brown eyes met his and she knew instantly he had called her down here to expose her scars even further. A sense of instant regret came over her. She should never have come down the stairs, she should have ignored him.

He walked towards her; his muscled body looked even better in the moonlight. His long green sweatpants showed his physique well and his sneakers didn't make a sound as he came nearer.

Unsure what his next move would be, she stood silently awaiting his approach. To her surprise, he took her into his arms and held her tight. Momentarily, she felt the need to fall apart and tell him all, but she quickly swallowed down the thought and released herself from his warm embrace.

The chairs were humid, but she didn't care. She sat down and stared at the wild ocean in front of her. The waves were mesmerising. The sound of the water slamming onto the sand and the ocean pulling back made her want to walk into the ocean and fall back into those waves. To get carried out onto wherever, that would be true serenity.

His eyes burnt a hole in the side of her neck, but she ignored him to the point where she couldn't stand it any more.

'What?'

'What happened to you?' His voice showed obvious sounds of melancholy. His facial expressions showed deep sadness, disappointment even.

It was that look she had dreaded mostly. The look of disappointment, as if she had done something wrong. Her heart rate was through the roof, almost overbearing the sounds of the waves. A layer of sweat shaped itself over her whole body. Her mind spun a million miles an hour, trying to find a way to control the damage.

There was no way he could find out all. She wanted to slap him, push him away, yell at him. Run off and never return. She did none of those things. Instead, she froze and watched, as in an out-of-body experience, he lifted up her left hand and turned it over.

She closed her eyes, shaking her right leg faster and faster. He knew, but he couldn't know. For the first time, someone saw the real her, and it was someone she cared deeply about. The shakes took control of her body as she began rocking back and forth in her chair, with him still holding onto her hand.

Her world had collapsed, the truth was out. There were no sarcastic or funny escapes any more. There was nothing she could come up with that would make this all go away. The stress reached her stomach. She got out of the chair and stumbled across the terrace. The inside of her stomach coloured the sand.
A brief moment later, she felt his hands on her shoulders, pulling her towards him. Towards safety.

***

The warm summer breeze made her feelings for him even stronger. It had been a long time since she had laughed that way.

Green leaves showed tiny shadows across the terrace. There were many people around, but she did not notice any one of them. She'd fought hard to not feel this way, to walk away. It was too soon, too wrong, and simply not the right timing. The watch she'd gotten from her offender still showed on her wrists, hiding a world underneath he would be afraid of knowing. Secretly, she had hoped she could tell him. Between the laughter, the warm smiles and the smitten eyes, there was an invisible barrier.

The wet glass touched the tops of her fingers and she dried them again on the paper coaster. He looked great, relaxed. Butterflies filled her stomach, and she had to look away from him. Sometimes, their eyes lingered too long. Too long for it not to mean something. Without saying a word, those brief moments told more than anything ever would.

Chapter 38

Our Father in heaven, hallowed be Your name.
Your kingdom come, Your will be done, on earth as it is in
heaven.
Give us this day our daily bread, and forgive us our debts as
we forgive our debtors.
Do not lead us into temptation,
But deliver us from the evil one.
For Yours is the kingdom, and the power and the glory forever.
Amen.

'Hello there, God, I'm slipping away again and I'm in desperate need a sign from You. Please guide me towards a place of excitement, as where I am now, there's nothing. Everything is the same and I am so tired. I can't stand this ordinary 'happiness'. I don't know how people do it. It's so quiet here and everything is tiring.

'I don't get how people think, how they live or what they live for. I want to drown myself in cutting, drinking and meaningless sex with people who don't deserve me. For a little while I was happy, I suppose, but I don't care for that 'happy feeling', it does nothing for me.

'So, today I picked up that blade again as soon as I had come home. There were no doubts, there was no guessing; it was the right thing to do. I didn't even bother having those yes-no or be-strong types of conversations with myself, because what I did was right. I had to do something to feel. Turns out happiness isn't my colour and I really do like colours.

'I really wish I could meet someone who would understand my brain. Someone I could talk to about the unexplained moments of intense sadness and tiredness. They just come around and I don't know why. Those voices especially annoy me when I have to focus — I just can't. It seems to be getting much worse…

'Perhaps I was never really happy at all. All I know is I want to get back to where I came from and need to get back on track with what I was doing, because that person felt layered. She was interesting, passionate. Do You know what I mean?

'The dullness makes me tired, but there are also these moments of extreme happiness. It's so annoying. There are all these people in my head when I get that happy. I can't seem to get them out. I like covering up my head when that happens, it stops some of the noise. Otherwise, writing helps, but not today; I am too tired. The cutting-high helped for a couple of minutes, I'll continue doing that. Hopefully, that'll give me some more energy over the next couple of days. I know I am disappointing You and the ones who love me, I just can't help it.

'How could I possibly stand out without those layers? I don't want to be ordinary. I hope You can forgive me.'

In the name of the Father,
The Son,
And the Holy Spirit.
Amen.

CHAPTER 39

'We welcome to the studio our news reporter, Mr Jack Binckle. Jack, what have you got for us today?'

Jack shifted in his chair, feeling annoyed. The previous time he had been called a former reporter for *The Times*, but now they knew he had something interesting to share, he had suddenly become *our* reporter.

'Right, first off, I am not one of your reporters. I freelance, thank you very much,' he spoke firmly at the female anchor. Apparently, they had thought it was better to place him with an attractive, blonde, female reporter.

The blonde faked a smile. 'Of course.'

Jack Binckle shifted his focus from the attractive woman into the camera. Appearance yes, brain no. Too much time had passed since the bombing, someone needed to tell the UK citizens the truth. It was his duty. From the corner of his eye, he could see the blonde shifting in her chair and uncomfortably trying to get within the camera's frame.

Jack Binckle knew all cameras were focussed on him, and only him. This was his moment to say what needed to be said. An exhilarating feeling came over him, it gave him chills. This was the kind of moment each rookie dreamt of in media school. To be the only one who knows the truth, and to have the balls to speak up and say just that. He took a deep breath and started his statement.

'Good morning, citizens of London, citizens of the United Kingdom and perhaps even citizens of the world. My name is Jack Binckle and I have uncovered the truth about the Underground bombing.'

He paused for dramatic effect, as if he was still brooding over his next few lines. 'Last night I was offered a bribe by Interpol. In specifics, by Director Kneebone and his assistant, whose name is unknown to me. I wasn't just offered a bribe; I was also threatened by them.'

His heart was racing and pounding in his throat, excitement with a touch of fear. Everyone in the room standing behind the cameras was intently eyeballing him. There were far more people in the room than was needed. He was clearly drawing an audience, and it made him want to put on a show.

'Interpol does not want you, citizens, to know that the man responsible for the Underground attack is still at large. Furthermore, Interpol has for some unknown reason not shared with you that there is a survivor. This survivor's identity is still unknown to me, but I can tell you it's a female who I estimate to be in her thirties and I have footage of her being in Turkey merely two weeks ago. Is this woman a part of the terrorist cell? Is that why

Interpol hasn't mentioned her? Or is she, in fact, a victim who Interpol does not want you to know about?'

Jack Binckle sat up straight and stroked his tie. Usually, he wouldn't have put one on, but this was a special occasion and he wanted to look his best.

'The lack of communication, all the victims, the survivor and an attacker still at large. Ladies and gentlemen, beloved citizens, we are at war with an unknown enemy.'

***

Jack Binckle rushed down the steps of the Channel 4 news building. The cool air played a trick with his glowing cheeks. Hot and cold. Proud and scared. He thought about it, over and over again as he rushed towards the stairway leading him to the Underground. There were flowers, teddy bears, cards and candles everywhere around it. Heavy security guarded the entrance and the inside of the Underground. As if anyone would be stupid enough to come back and plan another attack at the same place. But that's what they were good at, the police. Guarding *after* the damage had been done.

It would have been easier to lock down the entire Underground, but the economy needed it to continue to operate as much as possible and so the government had decided to keep it running until the next attack.

His blood was boiling as he continued walking through the Underground at a fast pace. He didn't realise he might look like a madman to some. Strangers' faces of utter panic went completely unnoticed as he walked past. He finally slowed down when he had to swipe his card before entering any of the platforms.

Declined. Declined again.

A police officer laid a firm hand on his shoulder. 'You appear to have insufficient funds on your card, sir. Please top-up before continuing.' He spoke calmly and gestured towards one of the machines in the corner.

There was a long queue and Jack Binckle was in no mood to wait. Annoyed, he pushed the officer's hand from his shoulder and ran back up the stairs, back into the cold air which still played a trick on his warm cheeks.

A taxi came near just as he exited the Underground and he flagged it down. He gave his address and the driver, an Indian man in his early forties, made clear he understood where that was in a heavy accent.

As he had finished his statement, the cameras had been shut down. The blonde female anchor had gotten up out of her chair without saying a word. After the cameras had been switched off and most of the staff had left the recording room, a man in an expensive suit had entered the room and taken a seat in the female anchor's chair.

'Mr Binckle, we haven't met, but I have heard a great deal about you. I'm a friend of Director Kneebone. I'm sure you know him?'

Jack Binckle hadn't replied. Instead, he had squeezed his eyes nearly shut and came to the realisation that he had made a huge mistake. His heart had dropped to the floor. He had just spilled all his intel and it was on camera. No doubt they'd use it against him now. He was in trouble, more so than before. How could he have been so stupid to not think twice? Of course Interpol's director had friends in the media.

The taxi dropped him off at his apartment building, but something told Jack Binckle it wasn't safe. Instead of entering, he went around the block and ordered breakfast at his favourite diner.

***

Patrick sat at his desk, awaiting Kneebone's first meeting of the day. Everything had gone back to normal, as far as that was possible. Patrick had picked up the coffee and opened the office, a few minutes later Kneebone had arrived and taken the coffee from him.

They had gone back to work as if nothing out of the ordinary had happened. It was important, Kneebone had said, to continue with their lives as they always had. Suspicious behaviour wouldn't help them one bit.

The small clock beside the computer showed the time as a quarter to nine. Only fifteen minutes to calm down and put on a straight face. He glanced over to the shut door and wondered about Kneebone's state of mind. Undoubtedly, Kneebone would be sitting quietly sipping his coffee and reading the paper. Possibly, he'd be preparing himself for the meeting by scribbling some notes into his diary, but that was unlikely. Kneebone's nine o'clock was a regular.

A low-key staff member of parliament who would come in every two weeks to get updates on cases, which he would later report back to his superior, and so on. There was not much to tell. The Underground bomber was still at large, and Agent Curtis hadn't gotten any closer to catching the man.

The calendar loaded as Patrick tried remembering the man's name. A few meetings throughout the morning, after that, nothing. Patrick wished Kneebone had been busy all day. The chances of him reopening their earlier discussion over lunch became all the more likely.

A man appearing in the doorway startled Patrick and he burned his tongue on his coffee. Clumsily, he put it down and cussed himself. The man, looking as bored and unimpressed as always, took a seat on one of the comfortable chairs near Kneebone's office door. Patrick did what he always did and used the small remote control to let Kneebone know his meeting had arrived.

Not long after, Kneebone pressed a button in his office, signalling to Patrick he was ready to receive his nine o'clock. Patrick held the door open and the man disappeared into Kneebone's office. Leaving Patrick an opportunity to disappear into the bathroom.

CHAPTER 40

IS IT SELFISH
TO ALWAYS BE
IN SURVIVAL MODE?

'What does it feel like for you?'

She looked up from the magazine she was reading. She wasn't sure what he meant, which must have shown on her face, because he immediately clarified his question.

'The darkness, I mean?'

'Oh,' she replied, quite taken back. 'I thought you meant the foot massage,' indicating she wanted him to continue.

'No, not the foot massage.' He smiled warmly, but not warm enough as a sign he wasn't going to let the subject go. 'I really want to understand you. I've never experienced those kinds of feelings.'

Outside, the sun had long set, but they hadn't closed the drapes. The few lights in the apartment offered just enough light for her to read her magazine. Only a moment ago she had thoroughly come to peace, sitting on the comfortable beige couch, reading a magazine on fashion as he rubbed her feet.

Even in a hectic city, they had managed to create a space where it was truly quiet. She had no idea how long they'd stay there, but she hoped it wouldn't be too long. Although she loved the feeling the apartment gave her, which she contributed to the fact that their living space was situated at the top floor of one of the highest buildings, she detested the busy city far below her. The apartment created a great escape from that hectic environment, but she had never been one to be bottled up inside the house all day.

'Why do you want to know?'

He stopped rubbing her feet, again. And she knew this time he wouldn't continue unless she stopped dodging his questions. Hoping they could move on from the subject quickly, she decided to give him a general answer. She put the magazine down and sighed.

'It feels heavy, but there're activities which help, so there's really not much of an issue.'

'Such as exercising and your writing?'

'Such as.'

She picked up the magazine again and hid her face behind it a little.

'I had a sister who suffered from the same.'

Surprised by his revelation, she put the magazine back down again, this time all the way onto the coffee table, but still close enough for her to reach it in case the subject got too real.

'Why didn't you tell me you have a sister?'

'Because I don't. I said I had a sister.'

His face expressed sadness and hurt. It was only there for a split second and she may have just wanted to see it, but she was strongly convinced he still thought of his sister a lot.

'I haven't seen you write in days.'

'I work on my diary when you're not here,' she fired back immediately, knowing he was coming for her.

'I have been here for the past few days. If you need time to work on it, then…'

'I did work on it,' she interrupted him.

'I don't believe you,' he replied without listening. It upset him, knowing she wasn't looking after herself. He knew he shouldn't force her, and he knew it might create the opposite effect, but his anger got the better of him.

His tone of voice baffled her and before she could utter a word, he started his outburst.

'I'm serious. You can't go around pretending you're fine and then burden yourself with all this. It's too insane…'

He got up from the couch and walked over to the window.

'And how dare you leave me to pick up the pieces!'

He turned around to face her again, his hands at his sides.

'You think you're your own happy self, but you're not. It's like you're incapable of functioning, and I don't have a clue on how to deal with it. If I knew what to do to help you… we could figure it out together.'

He walked over to the couch again and sat down, taking her hand.

'I can see you're in pain, but I have no cure, nothing to ease it. It frustrates me because you hold answers, but you won't give them to me.'

He looked her in the eye, his tone of voice had become softer and he rubbed his fingers across her palm.

'Tell me, please.'

His reaction scared her just as much as it irritated her. She pondered her response for some time; angry or obedient. Finally, understanding the severity of his concern and fearing what he'd do if she didn't tell him, she decided to go with the latter.

'I can't turn it off… The smallest efforts feel as if they are a complete workout. My entire body weighs a ton. And…' She leaned back and stared at her hands.

'And what?'

'I just don't care. About anything, anyone. Especially anyone. I wish everyone would just die so I don't have to pretend I'm happy.'

'Who says you have to pretend?'

'If I don't, people make fun of me. They think I'm just over-reacting to something that isn't there. They tell me to 'just be positive' or 'think positive'. If it was that easy, I would never feel down ever again. It's like nobody really cares. So why should I care? And then when someone does care… I just get so sad and I have to cry, and it doesn't get any better after that. Only worse.'

'I thought it helped to talk about it?'

'The only thing that helps is to sit it out and just wait for it to pass.' She paused, scraping together the courage to speak the next sentence. 'But sometimes it takes too long…'

'And then what do you do?'

'It depends on how much I love myself. I either turn to self-harm or self-love. Self-love is always harder, because I hate myself for being a burden to everyone around me. I hate myself for feeling this way because there's no foundation for it. There's no reason why I'm so depressed. And mostly, I hate myself for wanting everyone to die so I can have my peace. That's not okay. But it is really how I feel.'

Quietly they sat together, neither one of them knowing how to respond. As it turned out, neither one of them held the answers. So, without uttering another word, they sat on the beige couch, staring into the night and hoping it would pass sooner rather than later.

Chapter 41

Our Father in heaven, hallowed be Your name.
Your kingdom come, Your will be done, on earth as it is in
heaven.
Give us this day our daily bread, and forgive us our debts as
we forgive our debtors.
Do not lead us into temptation,
But deliver us from the evil one.
For Yours is the kingdom, and the power and the glory forever.
Amen.

'Hello there, God. Today I find myself missing my dad a lot… I wish to speak with him through You. I hope that's okay.

'I get it now, Dad. I recognise the same symptoms you showed. Only now, I see them in me. I'll be honest, it scares me. I'm sure you know — no offense — I do not want to end up like you…

'I notice I'm like you in the small things. Your inability to be around your family, your irritation when asked simple questions, your sense of powerlessness when small tasks go wrong. Your paranoia and mistrust of common people and things. Your absolute disregard

*for your own intuition. But mostly, your dark, sombre
aura.*

*'You carried that with you everywhere you went. It
always looked as if you weighed a hundred tons. Your
shoulders sagged and your arms hung alongside your
body as if they carried the weight of the world. You
always looked sad. Even when you smiled, your eyes
never quite matched. I can now see you were lying. To
the world, to us, but mainly to yourself.*

*'Each time we got home you would leave. At first, I
didn't understand. I mistrusted you and blamed you.
You never explained it, an apology never came. So, at
some point, to hide the pain, we started making fun of
you. At that time, I was unaware of the meaning behind
your absence.*

*'I get it now, because I feel the same way at times.
I just can't bring myself to sit in the same room as them.
I think it's because they're closest to me. I'm scared
they can take one look at me and see right through my
façade. They're trained and they know me. It wouldn't
be hard for them to figure out what I'm up to. Part of
me wishes they would, part of me wishes they will never
know. I don't know which side of me is braver.*

*'I would like to remain a mystery, to be partially
impenetrable forever, for anyone. I often wonder why I
desire to be impenetrable. Is it because I was hurt? I
would think, with enough time passing, that feeling
would pass. Or, at least, it would allow me to be my
complete self with a few of my closest people. But till*

this day, I haven't found anyone I could tell everything to, without getting judged or misunderstood.

'I mainly hide, create a diversion or simply lie, because I think people will interfere with my dreams. I think people won't allow me to be me if I told them who the real me is.

'I know who I am, I love who I am. I am, in a way, proud of my darkness. It makes me different and gives me a unique view of the world. Controlling the darkness, however, that is something I wish I could talk to someone about.

'If only I could find one person in this world who wouldn't judge me, someone who would just listen and accept. I won't go off a brink. I won't jump or kill. I won't go into a frenzy. All I ache for, is to be accepted within the darkest places of my soul.

'People broke me. I hate humanity. I'm not sure if that is normal, or if you felt that way. Strange enough, I don't think you did. I think there was a part of you which liked to be a social man. An outgoing, spontaneous kind of guy. It's a shame I never got to meet him. I'm sure I would have loved him to pieces.

'If I told you the darkest, most horrifying stories the voices tell me, would you listen? "Voices" is the wrong word, that's something for institutionalised people. They aren't a third party. They're me.

'If I told you the darkest, most horrifying conversations I have with myself, would you listen? I need you to stick around and listen to my dreams and

aspirations. Because those conversations I have with myself might sound creepy at first, but when you allow me to explain, they can bring magic to your life.

'I wonder why no one has ever asked me why I wear your ring. They all know of my difficult relationship with you. I suppose they consider it my way of keeping you close to me. I'm still wearing grandma's ring. I wear that because it reminds me of her. I treasure her ring and the memories it bears. Although I do not remember her wearing the ring, to me it symbolises the person she once was.

'It's quite the opposite for your ring. Yours bears a whole other meaning for me. No one knows it, but the small piece of silver on my thumb represents a life lost because of unspoken words. That's you, Dad. Your life was lost because of your unspoken words. You kept everything inside, bottled it up as if your life depended on it. I know it made you mentally unstable and sick, and I also strongly believe it gave you cancer. It's impossible to carry that much sadness, grief and heaviness inside you day after day without your body suffering from it.

'The path you chose for you is surely not the one I want to go on. Although I didn't see you suffer at the end of your life, I saw you suffer greatly throughout my childhood and youth. I never understood your pain. I did try to understand it, but growing up I just didn't have the insight. I'm sure you can understand that, and I hope you forgive me for it. I was only young, Dad, and

I saw too much pain in your eyes, it made me resent you. I didn't understand why you were in so much pain and why you refused to fix it.

'I understand your pain now and your difficulty in speaking up about it. Perhaps it was easier for me to choose a healthier lifestyle, because I do not have a partner and kids to worry about. If I took the time, I could fall apart and rebuild myself. I would have been more than happy to give you that time. I would have done anything to see the old you reappear.

'I miss you, Dad. I don't miss the sadness and difficulties you brought into my life, but I miss you as the person I knew you once were.

'If only we had a chance to speak all these unspoken words. I think it would make a massive difference. And I am so sorry I never got to see you happy. That was my wish, since I was a little girl.

'I hope you find your peace, because in that I will find mine.'

In the name of the Father,
The Son,
And the Holy Spirit.
Amen.

CHAPTER 42

The balance between embarrassment and pride,
darkness and light.
I think it will remain with me until I die.
For which I will have to fight,
not to let happen for a long time.

'Team.'

Kneebone walked in, addressing the both of them in one word as a manner of showing his authority. He kept his shoulders broad and gestured for Edmonds and Rowan to sit down. Curtis followed closely behind him and shut the door.

Kneebone took a seat at the head of the table and watched as everyone sat down on either side of the long, grey table. Nobody uttered a word and patiently waited for him to start speaking. He decided to showcase his authority some more as he, too, remained silent and looked around the room, carefully taking in each piece of evidence shown on the whiteboards; one of which would be his subject.

Edmonds spoke softly, unsure how to address the situation and wanting to make a good impression. 'Is there anything we can do for you, sir?'

Rowan looked at her, wanting to mimic her to keep quiet but her question had the desired result, as Kneebone replied.

'No, that's quite all right agent. I came here to inform you all of the latest developments in this case.'

Rowan watched Curtis intently. Kneebone's remark seemed to have had no effect on him whatsoever, it was clear that whatever Kneebone had come to say had already been discussed.

Kneebone coughed uncomfortably and quickly glanced over to Curtis. He secretly wished Curtis would tell the story himself, but he knew he wouldn't be the one to take the professional bullet for this one. And besides, letting Curtis tell the story to his team would render him coming down here unnecessary and that would potentially make him appear weak. He needed none of that. He scraped his throat one more time and began to explain the agency's side of the story.

'About seven years ago we had one of the most intelligent agents working for us, meaning Interpol.'

He paused to look around and see if anyone could somehow predict what he was about to say. 'This agent, a woman, was part of an elite team working cases everywhere in Europe. She was one of our best assets and closed some pretty big cases. Until… until she lost her mind.'

He knew he wouldn't make himself favourable with Curtis for adding that last part, but he needed to degrade her somehow. Curtis' face showed signs of anger, but he ignored it and continued.

'This female agent's partner was killed whilst on one of their undercover operations following a sex trafficking ring. She couldn't quite deal with the loss and rather than seeking professional help, she turned to alcohol and eventually drugs.'

He paused again and studied Edmonds' and Rowan's faces, purposely ignoring Curtis altogether. The two seemed to be listening intently, but were not sure on how any of his story had anything to do with their case.

'The alcohol and drugs took over everything within her personal life, and despite her best efforts of hiding her addiction, it inevitably came to light in a horribly public scene here at our headquarters.'

'How come we've never heard of her?' Rowan interjected.

Kneebone stood up from his chair as a way of regaining his authority, he hadn't expected anyone would interrupt his story with a question or comment.

'Because, agent Rowan, this was before your time. You've been on the force how long?'

Rowan, feeling uneasy with the strict tone of voice his director used, answered slowly, 'Ehm, about five years with Interpol now, sir.'

'Five years,' Kneebone chuckled. 'Yeah, I remember the days where I was still green. Good old days.' He stared out of the window for a moment, pretending to be reminiscing.

Rowan looked to his left, hoping Curtis would offer him some non-verbal explanation. But to his surprise his team leader just sat there quietly, accepting the strange behaviour.

'Anyhow. Like I said, this occurred before your time.'

'But still, I would assume I may have heard of this public scene she threw?'

'You haven't heard anything about it, because I didn't want you to.'

Kneebone stood next to Rowan, hands in his pockets, staring down at him. He wanted this man to keep quiet and accept *he* was the one in charge and no one else. The whole thing was a mess as is, but he wouldn't allow anyone to make fun of him for it.

'We made the decision to move her out of the agency,' he continued, walking in circles around the room. 'Of course, we didn't just let her go, we sent her to a treatment facility where she could get all the help she needed. Even offered to pay for it, but she wouldn't take this chance and turned her back on us, her family.' Kneebone felt unsure about what to say next and remained silent.

'But what does this have to do with our investigation?' Edmonds finally spoke.

Kneebone offered her a smile, but not a kind one.

'I was just getting to that.'

He took a deep sigh and sat back down at the head of the table. 'The woman who survived the Underground attack, the woman who we haven't told the world survived the Underground attack, that woman, is our former agent. And if she's here, she's here with a reason.'

Again, there was a silence. Rowan and Edmonds looked at each other, dumbfounded. 'You knew about this?' Edmonds redirected her anger at Curtis, as Rowan let her silence speak.'

'I understand you're upset.' Kneebone held his hands up in front of him as if it would bring down the level of annoyance within the team. 'But you have to understand it was in all of our best interest to see if her presence here at the Westminster station at that time had any connection to the person who planted the bomb.'

'Yeah, imagine the PR scandal that would create. I can just imagine the headlines: 'Former Interpol hero is the Underground bomber',' Rowan added sarcastically.

He was fully aware his director's eyes were shooting fire in his direction, but he ignored him and just shook his head in disbelief.

'You should have told us sooner. The both of you.' Rowan looked at Curtis, who looked straight back into his eyes.

'Hold on.' Edmonds tried keeping some of the peace and focussed on what was important. 'Are you saying there's a possibility she may have had something to do with this bombing?'

'Quite the opposite. We are saying she is the only one who can *help* us with the investigation. You've all seen the footage Flynn provided.'

Kneebone glanced over to Curtis, wanting to detect some sort of emotion. But he was wrong, and Curtis' expression stared back at him almost lifeless. Kneebone despised every moment he used to spend dragging Vanima further and further into his investigation. But the reality was, he needed her desperately.

'This information which I have just provided is strictly confidential. No one outside of this room is to know about this. No media, no other agents. Preferably, she herself also shouldn't know you are aware of this matter.'

Edmonds and Rowan looked at him, confused rather than scared or intimidated. 'You want us to question her, but leave out her past?' Edmonds asked, unsure if she had understood her director clearly.

'Quite right,' Kneebone nodded.

'How?' Rowan asked cynically.

'That's your problem. Not mine. Don't bring up her past as an agent. Do not discuss it with anyone else besides the people you see here in this room and Flynn. Am I clear?'

Flabbergasted, annoyed and confused, Rowan and Edmonds shook their heads.

'Great. I will see you later.'

'Just one second,' Rowan ordered, just as Kneebone opened the door.

'Yes, agent Rowan?'

'We don't even know her name.'

'Alexandra Vanima.' He turned around swiftly and walked out the door.

CHAPTER 43

The prime minister folded his hands and bowed his head, indicating the minute of silence had commenced. Thousands of people had gathered outside of what used to be the Westminster Underground entrance. The streets were covered with flowers, candles, teddy bears, poems and drawings. Pictures of the victims added the final piece of heartache to the scenery.

It surprised Kneebone this many people had shown up at all. Of course, it was normal for people to want to gather after such an event, but to have the gathering at a place all of London hated and had become frightened of, seemed contradictory to him.

If it was up to him to decide, the Westminster station would never be reopened. But he knew within the next couple of weeks some building company would start their works here and remodel it to the way it was, with improvements.

Hell, building companies would be fighting over the job. It would cost hundreds of thousands to get the station back to the way it had been, and any contractor out there would love to fill his pockets 'helping the citizens of London move on'.

The slim politician looked exhausted standing in the middle of the stage with his eyes closed. His pale skin showed he had been spending way too much time trying to come across as if he had the situation under control. He wasn't far away from retirement. Re-elections were just around the corner and with a disaster like this having happened under his ruling, it would be impossible for him to get re-elected.

Kneebone considered the thought of the PM secretly being rather happy about that. He was sixty-two years of age and had worked hard his entire life. Standing there in front of his citizens, the people who either admired him or despised him now, he seemed in over his head.

Underneath the clouds, a blue sky had emerged. As if God had wanted to apologise for the course of events and wanted to offer some peace for those attending the memorial service. Or perhaps He just wanted a front-row seat to see what mess He had created and didn't want the clouds to be in His field of vision.

Kneebone chuckled at the thought and then quickly maintained his posture. No one had seen it, as he scanned the crowd around him. Some people were crying, others stared into nothing, and the final group had followed the PM's example by closing their eyes and bowing their heads.

The sun offered some peace whilst the silence said more than any speech from a high-ranking official ever would. It reminded him of his grandfather's cabin, stacked away far up north, where he had spent the Christmas holidays as a little boy. The sun would reach their cabin in the early morning, but it would remain cold enough for the snow not to melt. Underneath the thick pine trees, small rays of sunlight would touch his face as he looked across the lake. If you didn't know any better, you'd think you were somewhere in Scandinavia.

Few people knew of the cabin, and the ones who did had always tried to buy it from his grandfather, who had lived there permanently. His grandfather would laugh at the offers people made him, protecting the one place where he could truly be himself.

Kneebone had admired that mostly in his grandfather and had always vouched to be just like him, but somewhere along the way he had gotten lost and the road to retirement in that cabin seemed to drift away further and further.

His family had wanted to sell it after his grandfather passed, there were too many good offers on the table. But Kneebone, barely having reached the age of eighteen, had fought to keep the cabin in the family; protecting it the way his grandfather had. Each month a part of his salary would go to the cabin, keeping the dream alive.

'Thank you.'

Around him, people sighed a sigh of relief or pain, scraped their throats and returned to a comfortable posture. It was over. The final act of remembrance had finished, until next year, when less people would show up to the memorial, and so on each year. Patrick's voice woke him from his thoughts.

'What did you say?'

'I said it was a good service. And I think the PM wants to speak with you. He's coming this way.' Patrick nodded in the direction of the PM, who was busy shaking the hands of people no one knew the names of.

'Director Kneebone,' the PM spoke when he had reached him as the men shook hands.

'Prime Minister. I must say it was a good service, I think people took comfort from your speech, sir.'

'Yeah, well, someone had to say something, right?'

'Quite right.' Kneebone felt thrown off by the low-key response and waited for the message the PM had for him, but to his confusion the PM remained silent. 'What is it I can do for you, sir?' he asked eventually, as he nodded politely to the people passing them.

'Not here. We will have to meet somewhere to discuss this situation. I will have my driver forward you an address and time for later this afternoon.'

'Oh, okay. Not a problem, sir.'

'No need to call me sir, we both know I will soon be gone from here.'

The conversation had become uncomfortable, and Kneebone couldn't hold in his curiosity much longer. 'Forgive my frankness, but what is this about?'

'Your witness, Kneebone. If she's truly the only one who could help us in this investigation, then it's time for us to come clean about what happened.'

Kneebone watched the PM's face intently as his superior continued to nod politely at the people passing him. His security guards, standing closely behind him, didn't flinch at what the PM had just said, and Kneebone wondered if they even knew what they were talking about.

For years the agency and parliament had forcefully covered up what had happened. Their work had paid off well and no one, except the inner circle, had found out about the occurrences.

'Sir, you are not thinking about…'

'Yes, I am,' the PM answered with such confidence Kneebone knew it would be impossible to talk him out of it. 'Look at me. I've got nothing left to lose. My wife passed away and my career will be over within the next couple of months. I've come to the realisation that I've made my fair share of mistakes. I turned my back on friends in the hopes of serving the greater good. But from where I am standing, there is no greater good. I mean, look at this place.' He gestured at the display of candles, flowers and teddy bears. 'It's time to make things right, and this will be my way of doing it. My driver will contact you and we will discuss the action I'd like you to take.'

Before Kneebone could answer, the PM had walked away, followed closely by his security team.

'What did he want?' Patrick's voice rose to the surface.

Kneebone turned around to face him. 'The PM made the decision for me. He wants to tell the world the truth.'

Patrick appeared stunned by this answer. 'Forgive me, but is he out of his mind?'

'It seems that way, doesn't it?'

'Do you think Jack Binckle has anything to do with this?'

'No, of course not. He's just some freelancer, there's no way he will ever be able to find out what happened, and there's no way he could influence the prime minister.' Kneebone twisted and turned, aware people were looking at him and knowing very well not to cause a scene. 'For heaven's sake! He's got to understand it's the worst idea. We've got to find a way to deal with his stupidity.'

'Wayne, keep your voice down. Come on, we're going to get some coffee and come up with a plan.'

Patrick returned to their small table in the back of the coffee house, holding two take-away cups. 'They don't start serving heavy liquor until four p.m.,' he joked.

Kneebone offered him a faint smile and removed the lid from his cup. 'We need to put an end to this. The world cannot, will not, know what happened to her. There's really no need for it. We don't even know if she saw anything.'

'But on the security tapes…'

'Yeah, yeah, the security tapes. She hasn't even come to yet. There's a chance she won't remember a thing, or better yet, there's a chance she will die without ever waking up.'

'Are you suggesting…?' He stopped talking as a small group of businessmen passed their table and leaned in closer. 'Are you suggesting murdering her too?'

'No, I wasn't. But that would work…'

'No, it wouldn't.'

'If she does wake up and he starts asking questions, who's to say she won't speak up about what happened?'

'I'm amazed she hasn't already.'

'She couldn't. We took care of that.'

'But how?' Patrick asked, realising he wasn't aware of all the details.

Kneebone shook his head, dismissing Patrick's interest in further details. 'What we need to focus on is finding a way to keep the prime minister from revealing to the public what happened. We can't kill her, there are too many eyes on us.''

'Then why kill Jack Binckle?'

'Because he is a loose cannon we can't control. We can control Vanima. Do we have something on the prime minister?'

'No, we don't. He's a widower and there's no speculation on gambling, alcohol or drug abuse. What you see is what you get.'

'Yeah, a wuss trying to make the world a better place by bringing hell to earth. We have to show him bringing in Alexandra Vanima, won't help us further the investigation. It would only distract from what's really important — finding the men responsible for the attack.'

Patrick took a sip of his coffee, which he found out was still too hot and he burned his tongue again. 'I think that is what he's after. A detour from the actual investigation.'

'Yes, but why? It would only make the agency and parliament weaker, and especially in a time like this, those two need to form a united front to both the country's citizens and its enemies. It makes no sense.'

'It does.' Patrick sat up straight. He had an epiphany. 'There's something he said to you earlier.'

'You overheard our conversation?' Kneebone asked, questioning himself how he felt about it.

A certain distance had always remained between the two men. A distance Kneebone would never agree to out loud, not to anyone. But Patrick could feel it at every function they attended. At times it had bothered him greatly, but he forced himself to put up with it, taking comfort in the knowledge that he had a job many would kill for with an almost certainty of financial stability for life. And besides, when he needed Kneebone, he did come through.

'You should be glad.' There was a shimmer in his eyes. He leaned in closer again before continuing, 'He told you, and I quote, "I've got nothing left to lose".'

'He was referring to his wife, and he's got no children.'

'I think he's dying.' Patrick smiled with excitement.

Kneebone, who was about to take a sip from his coffee, put his takeaway cup back onto the table and pondered the possibility.

'He did look awfully pale today, and slimmer. It could have been the cold winter air, or scenery of the flowers and candles, but he didn't quite appear to be himself.'

Kneebone still said nothing, wanting to be absolutely convinced before getting his hopes up. If it was true what Patrick was saying, it could be a great tactic to get him what he wanted — the witness out of the picture without having to get his hands dirty.

'My grandfather had cancer. Decided to not have any treatments like chemo or radiotherapy. I must say, the prime minister and my late grandfather share a similar physique. I'm speaking about the time a few months before his passing. He had that same peaceful, yet a little too peaceful, outlook on life. I'm not saying his will to live was over, but he had come to peace with the idea of dying. He went about his day like he always had, but he wasn't concerned any more. Quite like how the PM acted with you today.'

Kneebone, having heard enough to get him to start believing the possibility, finally replied to Patrick's epiphany. 'It's certainly a possibility. Once you say it, you can't quite unsee it. But I would need evidence. A report from his doctor, he must have gone to see an oncologist or pharmacist. He must be taking some sort of drug to relieve the pain. We need to investigate this matter further.'

'Perhaps there is a way we can still use Jack Binckle?'

Kneebone smiled. 'It's a possibility… My friend really scared him off, and I think he would be willing to do as we tell him now. And then…' He made a gesture with his hand, implying slitting his throat after they were done with him.

Again, there was that satisfying smile. Each time Kneebone talked about killing Jack Binckle, he had a smile on his face which almost made him glow. Kneebone had already reached out to a hitman, and Patrick was the one who needed to go and meet such a creature face to face as soon as the hitman had pinpointed a time and location. Just how Kneebone had been able to get in touch with him in such a short period of time was unknown to him, and he hadn't wanted to know. The further he walked beside Kneebone on this dark path, the more he realised there were much more layers to the man he thought he knew to his core.

'Great thinking, Patrick. Let's wait till the end of the meeting to contact Jack Binckle. I'll get a read on our PM first, and then we'll get Jack Binckle to investigate and leak whichever we need. I'll contact my friend so he can get him on-air time if needed.'

'We'll tell him to disregard the Underground investigation and bribe him with an exclusive file on the PM.'

'Excellent.' Kneebone nodded, convinced. 'We'll use him until we're done with him. These are the moments I realise why we are such a good team.'

It wasn't often Kneebone admired Patrick's suggestions. Most of the time he barely noticed all the hard work Patrick had to do behind the scenes to keep Kneebone's directorship running. And despite his friend's macabre side, Patrick felt a warm feeling come over him. The last couple of days had been madness, but now it felt like they were working as a team again.

'Great, I'll make it happen.'

CHAPTER 44

Unconditional love equals unconditional loyalty on both ends of the spectrum.

Seven storeys below Vanima, people passed in ant-like patterns. From up here they all looked so common. They looked like boring people, living boring lives. She hated that sort of sheep-like behaviour. She had tried all her life to stand out. If everyone was wearing or doing one specific thing, she'd not do or follow that purposely.

The previous night she had crossed another line. For a moment she had been able to escape the day-to-day struggles and pressure. Peace within the moment; everyone wanted it, but only few acquired it.

She reached for the pack of cigarettes and took out the last one. Annoyed, she threw the pack on the floor and inhaled the nicotine. It had started to rain. She didn't mind it that much. Rain over cold, any day. The smoke bounced off the window and danced around her a bit before evaporating.

It was a good thing she had disabled the fire alarm. A little trick her father had taught her before he had passed. He had been an absolute chain smoker.

Although she had stopped touching alcohol, she had always found it hard to resist the nicotine.

Marlboro Gold were her choice. When she had travelled for work and been on long flights, she had often pulled the same trick on the smoke detectors in the airplane bathrooms. Just once a stewardess had asked her about the cigarette smell. But without the fire alarm going off, there was not much for the stewardess to say. She had smiled warmly and retreated to her first-class seat. Her then partner had giggled and given her a fist pump before he had opened a file. They had discussed that case for many hours, keeping a muffled voice, and had skipped the airplane dinner they were offered. First class, business class or economy, the food remained disgusting.

Jean-Paul. Her first partner. She owed him her life, but he had gone too soon. A twelve-year-old child with a semi-automatic weapon.

It had taken a lot of sleeping pills to get rid of that image. *Twelve years old, where's this world heading?* The kid had been a part of a gang and been as dangerous as a serial killer. Jean-Paul's caring nature had wanted to protect the child, to talk him out of the gang and talk him into handing over the gun. But that was no twelve-year-old child. That was a killer.

She blew the last cloud of cigarette smoke into the room and dropped the cigarette in her left-over coffee.

CHAPTER 45

I showed you my deepest wounds.
You cared for them,
Healed them.
Then times got tough.
You stopped caring for them.
Times got tougher,
You tried to reopen them,
Tried to pour salt in them,
Expected me to succumb.
I survived.
Because
I saw it coming.

What happened to me?

She attempted to draw strength out of her pain, but her body remained lifeless and ugly. Her foggy brain did not tell her why she was unable to move, as she felt her heartbeat rising and pounding in her chest.

Again, she attempted to draw strength out of her pain. This time she managed to slightly lift her head. Her blurry vision only allowed her to see white walls and dark blue curtains. From the corner of her eye, she saw something sticking out of her mouth.

A male face, roughly forty years old, appeared above hers. The face expressed a concerned smile. He started talking to her, but she didn't understand what he was trying to say. It was as if he spoke a different language.

Suddenly, she felt his touch on her face and it frightened her. She didn't want him to touch her and so she moved her face to the left in the hope he'd stop touching her.

There was a woman, dressed in a white coat.

And then she remembered. The man, the briefcase, the deafening explosion, the pain — she remembered it all.

The sight of the woman next to her calmed her down and she was relieved to feel the pounding getting less.

The woman looked at the man, then back at her and made some sort of gesture.

She wants me to cough.

The woman repeated the gesture and she started coughing, keeping her eyes fixated on her. The long tube slid out of her mouth. A sense of relief came over her and she was even able to understand the words of the woman.

'Hi there, I'm Dr Tisley. We're so glad to see you're awake. I need you to remain calm and not move too much. You've been through a lot.'

The woman smiled warmly and slightly pushed a cup against her lips. She drank from it. It felt warm and it took her a second to realise it was water, but at least half of it fell down her chin.

'I'll go contact the agency. Will you stay with her?'

'Yes, of course.'

'Good. I'll be back soon and then we can do some preliminary tests with her.'

The fog started to disappear, and she was able to form a sentence.

'What happened to me?'

Her throat was sore and dry, and not all words came out the way they should have. She had no idea how long that tube had been in there.

'You were the victim of a terrorist attack in the Underground. There was a bombing.'

She remembered that part. The man, the briefcase, the explosion, screams, and then that deafening silence during which she had only felt pain. Her heart started pounding painfully again.

Dr Tisley watched the heart rate monitor. 'Do you remember anything of what happened in the Underground?'

'No,' she lied. She did not want to think about it. 'Was I in a coma?'

'Yes, we weren't sure you were going to make it. You're a strong one. In fact, you woke up a lot sooner than I thought you would.'

'Am I okay?'

***

'They called. She is awake.'

It remained silent on the other end of the line.

'I just, ehm… I just don't know what to say to her.'

Flynn was still unsure what to say, but he knew anything would be better than the silence he was providing his partner.

'You were never against her. That must give you some good grace.' He knew it sounded weak, but there simply wasn't anything better to say.

'I also didn't fight for her. I let her down just as much as the rest of the agency did.'

'No, you didn't.' Flynn sounded more confident this time. 'You didn't destroy her, you simply didn't have the power to go against what they did to her.'

'Still, I could have done more for her.'

'Well… On the off chance of sounding too melodramatic, perhaps God has granted you an opportunity to be her friend.'

Curtis sighed and rubbed his forehead. He knew Flynn was trying to look on the positive side of things, but truth be told, he was terrified of walking into that hospital now that she was awake.

The wrong which had been done to her was inhumane and he hadn't stepped up in the way he should have. Perhaps if he had, she would not have fallen as deeply as she had. And to make matters worse, hardly anyone in the agency knew what had happened to her. They had only witnessed her outburst when it had all come crashing down. Not even Flynn had known the story behind her breakdown. To the agency she was just an agent who had succumbed under the stress. Just another agent having a mental breakdown.

They had made fun of her, and he hadn't been able to do anything about it. He should have, but he had been sworn to secrecy. Now that past had returned home. And it had done so in a time of crisis.

'I don't know what to expect walking into that room.'

'I know...' Flynn remained silent again. He was still processing the information he had found in the classified files. Nothing could right the wrong, but he still hoped Curtis might.

'I just think... I just think you would be the best person to go and speak with her. There's no one else, Curtis. She won't trust anyone, and that might include you, but as of this moment she is our only lead. She is the only one who can identify the man carrying the bomb. We need her more than ever.'

'I know you're right. I just can't for the life of me think of a reason why she would be willing to help the agency which destroyed her.'

'Appeal to the agent-side in her. You told me she was one of your best, with an insane willingness to help people. That might just be enough for her to help you.'

Curtis sighed again. 'I hope you're right. Wish me luck.'

'You've got this, you always do,' Flynn spoke with a sweet, caring voice.

CHAPTER 46

Jack Binckle closed the door to his apartment building. He pulled the hoodie of his raincoat further over his head and started walking towards a convenience shop, about a block from his apartment.

An Indian man in a bright blue turban gave him a small nod as he entered, before returning to a football match shown on a small television set near the counter.

Jack Binckle strolled down to the refrigerators at the back of the store and lay a carton of milk and some bacon in his basket. He then walked aisle per aisle and added all items he thought necessary to keep him fed for at least the next three days. A loaf of brown bread, some eggs, a couple of bags of nacho cheese crisps, several cans of tomato and basil tuna, some crackers and frozen pizzas.

The last stop before leaving for his temporary residence was the liquor shop, where he bought two bottles of whiskey. A good fifteen-minute walk later, he arrived at an old building in a regular street on the outskirts of London. The mailboxes beside the main entrance were dirty and most of them had flyers sticking out of them.

The long stairs, with green, worn-down carpet, led him to the second floor of the building. The door opened with a creaking noise as Jack Binckle looked around the hallway to make sure he wasn't followed. Quickly, he pushed the door further open and rushed inside. The room was dark, and he left it that way.

The hide-out consisted of one room, which served as both the living area as well as the bedroom, with an adjacent bathroom and a small kitchenette. This would be the place where he would uncover the truth about the Underground bombing and, he hoped, the sole survivor. He placed the groceries inside the small fridge and took a glass from the shelf into which he poured his whiskey. He then sat down on the dark green sofa bed and stared at the wall across from him where a hideous painting of a girl hung a little crooked.

Nobody in the media had mentioned her name or captured a picture of her. The media and the police had issued no statements of any survivors. Only Jack Binckle and Interpol appeared to know of her existence. Jack Binckle couldn't help but shake the feeling the girl in the hospital bed was the answer to all of it, whatever her story was. The police would have loved to show such a thing as a survivor; it would be considered good press. They could use her knowledge to make themselves appear stronger and they could use the positivity of a survivor. One survivor sounded better than forty-seven dead. Yet, the whole world had remained silent about her.

Suddenly, a thought crossed his mind. The doctors who had looked after her right after the bombing would have had to have known more about this woman. They were the only ones outside of Interpol who knew she had survived, but none of them had spread the word. Thoughts rattled through his mind and only created more questions than answers.

He got up and took his camera. He zoomed in on her picture and took a closer look at her face. Small scratches were carved into her cheeks and forehead. The incubator covered her mouth, and he followed it down her body. Focussing on both arms, he didn't discover anything relevant; no tattoos, just more cuts. Sheets covered the rest of her body, but still showed an obvious misshape.

Quickly, all scenarios ran through Jack Binckle's mind. If she had died, she would be a dead end for him. If she had survived, but was still in a coma, he could visit her and read her charts. If she had survived and was now awake, she would undoubtedly need physiotherapy. The ideal place for him to sneak in when things had quietened down a bit.

The last sip disappeared, and Jack Binckle decided it was time to set up. He pulled out his laptop and opened a surveillance program. Slowly, the footage loaded as he activated all cameras. He refilled his glass, popped another pill and sat down to watch the footage of his own apartment.

Kneebone's black SUV pulled up to a remote location he had only heard rumours about. The old ruins of what used to be a castle were about an hour drive from Interpol's HQ. The cold wind immediately took possession of his willingness to get out of the car, but as he spotted the prime minster, he knew it was too late to turn around.

The instructions had been very clear — come alone and tell no one where you're headed. Of course, Kneebone had immediately informed Patrick of the place and time of the meeting.

Kneebone looked around. There was no other car beside his. It made him wonder if the prime minister's driver was hiding somewhere, watching the meeting. A cold chill rolled down his spine. A chill he told himself was the result of the cold weather, even though he knew better.

It wasn't normal to meet at such a remote location to speak with the PM alone about a case which had occurred years earlier. There couldn't possibly be a good ending to this meeting, and the thought of it being a perfect spot for a liquidation ran through his mind. But as he walked closer to the PM, he couldn't find a reasoning behind that fear. There was no way the PM would benefit from a dead Interpol Director at this stage, even if he was dying and personally held him responsible for what had happened.

The cold wind pulled on his clothes and he realised it was possible the PM hadn't even heard him arrive. The wind roared louder than the engine of his SUV had. Kneebone stood still a few feet behind the PM, watching his back and taking in the posture while he had the chance. The man standing in front of him was indeed slimmer than he had seemed a few months ago.

Just as Kneebone was about to scrape his throat as a way of announcing himself and not to startle his superior, the PM turned around and looked him straight in the eye.

'Thank you for coming, Wayne.'

The first-name basis threw him off and it took him a moment to recover. 'Yes, of course, Prime Minister.'

'Oh, please, we are not here for that. I want this to be an informal meeting between two friends who will be working together. Call me Sam.'

An informal meeting between two friends, discussing what could potentially be a case of national security. It wasn't just out of the ordinary, it was far beyond protocol. But, as always, Kneebone did as he was asked by his superiors.

'Okay then, Sam.'

'Believe it or not, but this property, or what's left of it, was once owned by my ancestors.'

The PM walked closer to the ruins. The thick, green grass had conquered the entire area as far as their vision stretched.

'This used to be a castle, on the top of this hill. It's magnificent, isn't it?'

'It is indeed, sir. I mean, Sam.'

The PM smiled and continued his story. 'We're standing where the drawbridge once used to be. You see left and right, this ditch is where they used to have the water. My ancestors at some point removed the drawbridge and replaced it with this slope of sand and rocks, creating a connection between the castle and the hill without needing the bridge,' the PM pointed out as he told his story.

Kneebone listened intently, nervously waiting for the real story he had come to hear. He didn't care for this type of storytelling. In his experience, those types of stories were always an introduction to something far more serious and intimidating.

'I can see you're not interested in hearing the rest of my story.'

'No, no, please continue.'

The prime minister laughed. 'Relax, Wayne, I'm not here to kill you. Politically or otherwise.'

Kneebone forced a smile and walked a few steps away from his superior, pretending to take in the surroundings.

'I brought you here to tell you I am dying.'

Kneebone looked at him in shock. Even though he had suspected it, it was still quite a horrific discovery. It also meant his leverage went out of the window.

'Cancer. Stage three. Can't do anything about it any more. They've given me a couple of months.'

The prime minister smiled kindly at his colleague and then turned his head to face the ruins again. 'God, this place is magnificent. I hope, when I am gone, I'll get to wander around here and enjoy the sun.'

Kneebone eyed him from the side, feeling uncomfortable with the wishes his prime minister expressed.

'I have decided to give that girl what she needs. Whatever it is, she should get it.'

'I'm sorry… You are referring to Vanima, are you, Sam?'

'Yes. Alex.'

The use of the first-name basis for an agent he had never met, threw him off even more. There was no reasoning any more with the man standing beside him. He was looking death straight in the eye and didn't seem to be scared. Nothing Kneebone or Patrick could come up with would top that. The only thing he could do was to keep the man running the country in his close perimeter.

'I think that is very kind of you, sir. Sam. What exactly are you thinking of giving to her, so to speak?'

'Anything she wants. I'm thinking she will ask to be reinstated. And if she does, we'll give it to her.'

Kneebone didn't reply, feeling angry at the level of stupidity being portrayed by a man many looked up to in times like these.

'I can see you don't agree, but I don't care. She suffered because of you, Wayne. What you did to her is unspeakable. You are lucky it happened before it was my term, because I would have ended you.'

An even colder chill ran down Kneebone's spine. He had never had anyone speak to him like that in his entire career.

'This is your opportunity to right a horrible wrong. I suggest you do so, or my last deed as prime minister, will be to de-classify that file and make it public.'

Without saying another word, the prime minister walked away and got into a Mercedes which had just pulled up. Kneebone stayed behind, feeling nothing but cold.

CHAPTER 47

I prefer to stay broken.
Wouldn't know who I'd be,
If I healed me.

'You okay?'

'Yeah, just having trouble focussing.' Vanima's voice trembled as she slowly moved around the room. She couldn't go any faster, the body in which her sick soul lived would collapse to the floor. The dizziness made each move unbearable. Her mind was restless and incapable of sitting still, millions of things passed through her mind.

Breathing was hard. It took everything within her to not start hyperventilating. The pressure on her chest… it made her want to lie down and sleep, but her mind wouldn't allow it. The heart palpitations, God they were so painful, and scary. Having a heart that's nearly beating out of your chest might sound like fun, but it was painful. Anxiety is the word society used for it.

And then there was the having to pretend as if she wasn't just about to hit the floor, as if her body wasn't aching all over and as if her sick mind was giving up. Exhaustion.

And the vicious circle continued.

'Are you sure you're okay?' her colleague asked her again.

'Yeah, all good. Just going to get some fresh air.'

Please just leave me alone. I can't hide this much longer.

She rushed past her colleague, her eyes staring into nothing. Her beautiful brown eyes were looking but no longer seeing. Similar to the way people treated mental health at the agency.

Coming out and saying you suffered from panic attacks was a taboo. Hiding that by overmedicating was brave, and an unwritten rule. Dealing with addiction, that was for losers. There was nowhere to turn. Her life would be over if she was to say something. She wouldn't be able to oversee the consequences. No, she just needed some 'air'.

You okay? The phrase kept playing over and over in her mind. If only society didn't dictate that 'Yes, how are you?' type of reply… how different the world would look. She wasn't okay, she knew she wasn't. But who would care enough to do something about it? Personally, she couldn't, not any more. The only thing standing in the way of looking after herself was the fact she thought she was unworthy of the self-love. She didn't deserve it. And unless someone was going to realise she truly wasn't okay and make an effort to save her, she wasn't going to stop.

The bathroom stall. Her safety harbour. Her place where she could hide and be the real her. The addictive personality loved that stall. It was familiar. Pills rattled as she shook some out of the bottle and into her hand. The shakes had started to become uncontrollable, and two took a dive into the toilet bowl.

Fuck.

The door opened and footsteps approached the stall she was in. She stared at the pills in her hand and wished for the person to go into a stall. They passed and went into the stall next to her. Quietly, she swallowed the pills and felt a vague ecstasy come over her. An ecstasy others called 'relaxation'.

CHAPTER 48

I didn't realise who I had lost, until I had come back to myself.

Vanima glanced over to the person standing in the door opening. It was clear he was hesitant on whether he should enter her room. She wondered what she'd prefer, but she ultimately knew she didn't have the power to decide. Her head started pounding, as did her heart. This was a moment which was long overdue. She was the one in charge here, but her physical state didn't allow her to feel that way. Still, she felt a lot stronger than she had the last time she had faced him.

He had decided and cautiously stepped into her room, closing the sliding door behind him without barely making a sound. He turned around again to face her.

Pain, sorrow, regret and uncertainty. Those were things she noticed he felt, or hoped he felt. She wasn't going to be the first one to speak, not because she didn't have the confidence, but because she had spoken so many truths before and no one had cared enough to listen. It was his turn to wait on her, it was his turn to beg her, it was his turn to wonder whether he could live with himself. Eventually, he spoke, so soft she could barely make out the words.

'How are you doing?' His voice trembled, he had to scrape his throat.

She had often envisioned this moment, but not with him. With a higher-ranking scapegoat. Someone who had deliberately pushed her traumas aside to gain status. Momentarily, she worried she might feel sympathy for him, but she was relieved to notice she felt absolutely nothing. If anything, her heart had returned to its normal rhythm and the pounding in her head had subsided.

She gave him an ice-cold look as a reply.

He looked away, to the tips of his shoes, and scraped his throat again. He knew there was nothing he could do to make any of it better. He completely and utterly depended on her kindness after all the traumas he hadn't cared enough to heal. He should have stepped up for her, should have helped her, should have reached out. But he hadn't. Truthfully, he hadn't dared. Regret and sorrow had filled him to the point where he simply couldn't even think about the event any more without severely loathing himself. And the more time had passed, the more he had started to hope he'd never have to pay for his mistakes.

He took some steps in her direction, gaining ground. She didn't move, didn't flinch, but continued looking at him. Nearly looking through him.

'I should have…'

'But you didn't,' she was quick to reply.

He nodded, his head again falling to watch the tips of his shoes. He lifted his head and looked outside.

'I can't even begin to… I mean… Yeah… There's just nothing I can say to make any of it any better. You probably can't even stand the sight of me.' He followed the latter with a soft, self-demeaning chuckle. 'I came here to see if, despite all we have done to you and haven't done for you, you'd be willing to help us with this investigation.'

He looked at her, expecting a range of anger, sadness and disapproval. But her facial expressions didn't change.

She felt nothing for him, she had thought she would if she ever was to see him again. He had been the best of the worst, but still he hadn't done enough for her. He hadn't understood just how badly that life 'experience' had altered her life. How it had caused everything to derail.

Inside, she fought a battle, whilst maintaining an emotionless exterior. She had hoped the agency, or any agency, would ask her to help with the investigation. Despite it all, she had even memorised her demands, but now she had gone blank.

'I'm okay,' she decided to reply. Buying herself more time to run over his request.

'Good, good,' he replied immediately. 'I'm glad you are okay…' He knew he had to continue. If this moment passed there might never be another. 'For what it's worth, I am incredibly sorry for what's happened to you and I just wi-…'

'I don't want to talk about it.' A grim reply, enforced by a stern look.

'Okay, okay. I understand. But if you do… I am here. Now. I am here now.'

This was the part she had always liked about him, the part where he pushed through with victims because he knew how to read them. He knew she needed someone to talk to and he knew she needed to know. But the trust was gone. Not necessarily in him, but in all humankind claiming to be there for another.

'If I do this…' she spoke slowly, carefully considering each of her words, 'I have certain demands, which are not negotiable.'

He looked up at her, feeling so flabbergasted at her willingness to help that he couldn't even shape a reply at first.

'My demand is to be reinstated as an agent. Full clearance.'

He nodded slowly, pondering a way to give her what she wanted. 'I'm not sure if…'

'Like I said, it is not negotiable.'

He nodded, unsure whether he could deliver. 'What else?'

'I will deal with the past in my time, in my way. There is to be no one interfering with that.'

He nodded again, scared of what she had in mind.

'And last, but not least; I am to be on your team.'

'Okay… I will have to get approval for that from higher up the tree. As I am sure you are aware.'

'Painfully aware,' she sneered.

He nodded again, feeling less self-conscious. The fact she was willing to help showed him there was still something there which could be fixed. And now, he would have the time for it.

'Thank you. I will let you know what they decide.'

He turned around and opened the door. there was no point in staying any longer, she clearly didn't want him to. And yet, he wondered.

'If you don't mind me asking.' He turned around again to face her. 'Why are you agreeing to help us?'

She looked him in the eye. 'Because I am the only one who can identify him. I saw him, Curtis.'

***

'Flynn got us the access we need. The facial recognition software is running all over Europe.' Rowan walked back into their office, carrying two laptops. He handed one to Edmonds and sat down.

'I was thinking… It just seems like this is all too much of a coincidence. I don't mean to discredit Curtis in any way, but I feel as if he's blind to seeing what's in front of him.'

'Sounds an awful lot like discrediting him,' Rowan mumbled. 'But I can't say I disagree. There is much more to this story than they told us.'

He glanced over to his colleague, who was busy reading the forensic report on the dead Middle Eastern male they had found.

'Between us?' he asked for her discretion.

She looked up. 'Yes?'

He laid a small, yellow piece of paper on the table. 'I bet you that's the code.'

Edmonds looked stunned, but intrigued. She slowly grabbed the paper and typed the survivor's name into Interpol's system.

'They can trace it,' Rowan reminded her.

Edmonds ignored him and typed in the password as Rowan moved his chair closer to hers.

'We're in.'

They shared a look of excitement.

'That one.' Rowan pointed at a classified file marked 'Incident Report'.

'I'm going to print it, just in case they change the password.'

Rowan nodded and walked over to the printer.

As they lost themselves in the files, they both reached the same conclusion; she had truly lost her mind somewhere along the way, which would make it impossible to trust any of her statements.

CHAPTER 49

I used the knife,
I had bought for protection,
to harm myself.

Vanima lay awake and stared at the ceiling. She overheard a couple entering their motel room next door, they had been drinking. The joy, the shushing and the passionate kissing easily penetrated the thin walls.

She went back to her own thoughts, thinking about the most painful death known to mankind, and contemplating reasons as to why it was so. Suicide doesn't kill overnight. It doesn't decide you won't wake up any more from a nap or for your skull to be crushed in a car accident. It takes years of darkness for it to finally kill you. And whether the death itself was truly painless, no one would ever be able to tell.

Her leg hurt, more than usual. Sleeping was not a possibility and it hadn't been for a long time. The bottle of sleeping pills on the table a few metres away from her were calling out.

Take us, it'll make the pain go away.
But how many to take for all the pain to go away?

She slowly moved her legs and got herself seated in bed. The crutches lay beside her bed, awaiting their next use of assistance. The pills rattled in the orange plastic cylinder. Miss Alexandra Vanima, the label said.

Will you take me, to be your lawfully encouraged addict in sickness and in health? Yes.

She struggled to make it to the mini fridge located next to the door and took out a bottle of water. The pills went down with ease, something she wasn't used to, but something she had noticed had become easier. The thought of taking the whole bottle at once ran through her mind momentarily.

She covered herself up with the warm sheets again and wondered whether they were clean. The stain in the ceiling at which she had been staring slowly started disappearing as her eyelids grew heavier.

She had never been in this city and yet she felt strangely at home. Homesickness was something she had struggled with most when travelling for work. Especially at night. Now, with the recent events, she hadn't thought much of home, which was strange. Most people, when experiencing trauma, would love nothing more than to return home, to their safe harbour.

But Vanima had nowhere left to run, she had become estranged from her family through traumas and deaths. Home for her was the agency. Her work was her life. The journey she was on, finding his killer, gave her a new goal in life. It gave her a reason for enduring the pain she was in. It also gave her a reason to not swallow all those pills at once.

'You are not drinking because your life is out of order. Your life is out of order because you're drinking.' Vanima rubbed her eyes. Her partner had told her that once. It had taken her a little while to understand it and to trace that quote back to her own life.

At first it had seemed like a quote only meant for the hardcore addicts. But the longer she thought about it, the more sense it made. It offered her a certain perspective into her own life. It offered her a way out of that gnawing feeling trying to get her to pop more sleeping pills, trying to get her to drink. That temptation to feel high, to feel like she was floating. That gnawing feeling had somewhat gone away. Or at least, she now understood it. And understanding it had made it easier for her to deal with.

I'm not taking sleeping pills because I have a hard time sleeping. I'm having a hard time sleeping because I'm taking sleeping pills.

It made sense, and keeping that in the back of her mind had helped her tremendously. Each time she had wandered off onto the brink of relapse, she had always gone back to that quote, and it would bring her straight back. It had even allowed her to drink socially. To drink when she felt mentally strong to withstand the thought of getting wasted throughout the following days.

Since she had stopped taking those pills and decided to only drink socially, her life had improved a great deal. She had been able to sort out some of her mental health issues and was doing much better.

Then he had died, and everything had changed. How could she deal with that empty, black hole within her without something to make it go away? She couldn't do that by herself. She needed someone to stay with her and hold her hand.

CHAPTER 50

The rain poured down, but it didn't seem to bother the pedestrians in London's busy shopping district. Here and there, store owners had hung up signs showing they were supporting all victims, but none of them had closed.

Contemplating thoughts of self-hatred, Patrick kept on walking. His shoes made squeaky noises on the wet stones. He should have brought an umbrella, but he hated carrying one and so he had decided his hoodie would have to do. The London weather was the main reason he had longed to leave the country for some time. But unconditional loyalty had kept him right by Kneebone's side. All the way to murder.

He knew he should have said no, because it was never going to be over. Still, he had gone out without any form of protest. His stomach twisted and turned as he neared the little café with the red signage. The story inside that tiny, vintage-looking café would undoubtedly change him for life. He could still turn around, walk away an innocent man. Someone who had had a change of heart, a good Samaritan.

But the vision of returning to Kneebone without a job well done was unbearable. There had been something in the glance of Kneebone's eyes, or rather the missing thereof, which scared him. His friend's and boss' eyes had emptied out since that poker night. There was a certain chill to them now. He'd experienced that chill in those eyes before, but it had never been directed at him.

This time it was, and his eyes were emptier than ever. So empty, Patrick wondered if they'd ever be filled again. No one could stop him, not his wife, not other friends or colleagues. It was up to Patrick to get the job done or talk him out of it.

A small yellow light lit up the entrance to the café. A little pool of water had formed itself underneath the rack used to hang umbrellas. Relieved to be inside and out of the rain, he ignored his stomach's intuition and walked up the chestnut-brown, wooden stairs.

Almost there, almost no way out any more.

As he continued up the stairs, he could hear soft music and laughter. Only the laughter didn't fill the room. It made sense, as it was too early for most people to be in a bar. The sound of a pool table attracted his attention. The men surrounding it ignored him as Patrick watched them intently. It couldn't be any one of them — they were too relaxed and not alone.

A lone bartender in his late forties gave him a small nod as he continued polishing the beer glasses and preparing his bar for another busy night. It was ridiculous, he knew, but every single person inside the bar appeared in his mind as an undercover agent. The way they looked, talked or ignored him. It was all suspicious.

He kept on walking. In summertime, students, hardworking business people and tourists would fill their upstairs terrace. But for now, a sign saying, 'Our apologies for the inconvenience, but our terrace is closed today', prevented him from having an unobstructed view of the street.

He glanced around the café and noticed a lone man sitting at one of the small tables. Again, he looked around, over his shoulder, ensuring there was no one else sitting alone at a table. What a fiasco it would be to approach the wrong person.

There was no one else who matched his imagination's stereotype of a hitman. Besides, there was only one man wearing a black turtleneck, which was the one identification mark the hitman had told him about.

Suddenly, he realised he was still wearing his hoodie and he quickly took it off, feeling like an idiot. He looked around one more time, locating all the exit routes. One was the way he had just come, and one was through the kitchen. But that route was unknown to him.

He would have preferred to have an unobstructed view of the exits, but the way the hitman had already taken that seat, leaving Patrick with an empty chair facing the closed-off terrace.

He walked over to the table, the music behind him slowly disappearing with each step he took. The people in the café looked at him, all of them had their eyes trained on him and they started shaping a circle around him as he got nearer. Or so it felt.

The hitman himself must have noticed him approaching, but he pretended he hadn't and quietly continued reading the menu.

Unsure of what to say, Patrick stood beside the table and lay down Jack Binckle's photograph, one in which he was smiling and looked like a well-established professional. Kneebone had found the picture somewhere online, where someone had posted it alongside an article about Jack Binckle's success on a report about human trafficking. Sure, the interview was several years old, and the man had aged since, but Patrick struggled with the fact of handing such a happy photograph to such a dark persona.

The hitman looked up, as if he was disturbed by his company.

Patrick knew he must have annoyed the hitman for showing up like this, and not greeting him in some way. Then again, any kind of greeting would have gone horribly wrong. His heart beat so loud, he wondered whether the people around him could hear it.

'So, this is the man?'

The hitman took a good look at the picture. The voice was masculine, but not as heavy as Patrick had expected.

'Y-y-es, that is him. H-h-he's a reporter and he's making our lives a living hell.'

The hitman seemed uninterested in any information, except for the absolute necessary facts.

'You can keep the photograph.'

The hitman gave him a wondering look, making Patrick even more uncomfortable. 'Pardon me, I haven't really done this before.'

Again, a penetrating look.

'Would you sit down already? You're creating unneeded glances from the people here.'

The hitman spoke with a certain irritability in his voice, but his demeanour remained calm as to not arouse any suspicion from people present in the small café.

On a normal day, Patrick would have loved this kind of place. He would bring a book and enjoy a hot tea or a special beer, depending on the time of day. He could picture himself sitting outside on the terrace feeling completely relaxed.

But when he looked back to the hitman, he realised this was the most unusual situation to be in. He looked even more threatening now that he was on the same level, sitting across from him. Again, he looked towards the exit, assuring himself it was still there.

When he was still standing, he had a clear escape route. But now the hitman was blocking his way. All he had to do was get up, put his hands around his neck and it would be game over. Patrick shivered at the thought and attempted to cough it away.

'You really need to relax, or I am walking out of the door. You are starting to draw attention to yourself.'

Patrick nodded nervously and shoved his hands deeper into his coat's pockets, which was still wet from the weather outside.

'Hi, what can I get you gents?'

Patrick looked up and into the smiling face of a blonde waitress. He didn't notice anything else about her, except for her warm, and more importantly, safe energy. He managed to smile back and felt some stress fade away.

'Two coffees, please, for me and my friend. Thank you.' Demonstrative, the hitman handed back the menus and nodded friendly at the waitress.

'What other information do you require?' Patrick had found his voice again and eased his clenched fists, still hiding away in his coat pockets.

'Take off your coat and pretend you're having a good time.'

Another order, which he obeyed immediately. His eyes searched for the friendly waitress and he found her behind the bar. She was still here, and all was going to be okay.

'Thank you. Now I can tell you what I require from you.'

The hitman's voice demanded his concentration again and he looked back into the cold, blue eyes. The man was older, he realised now. Heavy build, small lines around his eyes and on his forehead, and very masculine. No doubt he would have tattoos, hidden away under his black turtleneck. But the man's pale skin took some of the intimidation away.

'This is how I work.' He paused as the waitress placed two warm cups of coffee between them and he thanked her. As soon as she walked away, he continued his story. 'I require a fifty percent pay-out up front and a fifty-percent pay-out after the job is done.'

'But how will we…?'

'I will send you a photo.'

'But won't that…?'

'Untraceable, because we will use burner phones, you will purchase me one and deliver it to me here.'

The hitman slipped him a napkin across the table with a location, not an address.

The manner of his answering made Patrick realise once again this wasn't the first time the hitman had been asked these questions. Despite the terrifying situation, Patrick admired the way the hitman could keep his cool.

'I have information on you. So, if this is a set-up, then you know you are not safe. There are only two reasons for me to kill: money is the first, and the second is to keep my career safe and out of sight. If your knowledge of me and my business is a threat to me, then I become a threat to you.' He paused, took a sip of his coffee, and then added, 'And your boss, of course.'

'M-m-my boss? How do you…?'

The hitman chuckled; the innocence of his clients never ceased to amaze him. 'I do my research. And besides, you give away much too much of yourself. You said, 'He makes *our* lives a living hell'. You didn't say '*my*', you said '*our*'. Clearly indicating this isn't a one-man show. Then there's the nervousness on your part; you don't strike me as the leader-type, but more so as the underdog-type.'

Patrick frowned and leaned back into his chair. He was insulted, but too scared to say anything in return. Besides, there was also a part of him which knew the hitman was right.

'Where can we bring you the money?'

Patrick wanted to move on from the uncomfortable statement. The coffee had cooled down enough and he started sipping it quickly, wanting it all to be over sooner rather than later.

'There will be a bank account number in an envelope on that location. You transfer fifty percent into that account. Once I have received the money, I'll start working. The second payment will be done into a different account. Which you will receive after my job is done.'

'Okay.' Patrick nodded along convincingly.

'Thanks for the coffee,' the hitman said, as he put the cup back down.

Before Patrick could utter another word, the hitman walked out of the café, leaving Patrick feeling in shock as well as relieved. He got up and paid for the two coffees, leaving the blonde waitress an extra-large tip. She seemed confused, but didn't protest and kindly thanked him. Patrick smiled back and walked out of the door as quickly as he could.

Once outside, he realised it was still raining, and now the wind had picked up, too. He smiled a broadly and inhaled the cold, horrible weather, feeling relieved he had made it outside again. Without bothering to put his hoodie back up, he decided to walk back home to calm his nerves.

CHAPTER 51

Jack Binckle knew he was closing in on the truth. The woman in the hospital bed wasn't just any survivor; he had uncovered her identity.

On-air time wasn't an option any more. He needed to get the truth out through a different medium. The blog which he had started had now finally attracted the number of readers he had wanted.

Another gush of whiskey warmed his throat. His ex-wife had rung him another ten times. He had ignored her just as many times and instead had poured himself a few drinks.

There was no point in stopping now. They had already decided he was a problem, and he knew his integrity wouldn't allow him not to go through with it. His next post would attract international attention.

He stacked his printed papers and used a stapler to keep them together. It was nearing three a.m., but he had done it. Those printed words on those few A4 pages would open up people's minds to the possibility of the government lying to them. It would make them think.

His favourite college professor had once told him the goal of journalism — to make people *think*. Telling people the truth, was one thing, but making them think was something completely different, as his professor had explained; there is no truth, only perception.

A couple of decades ago, the newspapers had been more objective. They had given the world the facts. Nowadays, the world of journalism was changing, and every newspaper, media station or reporter wanted to make money. Their integrity was slowly disappearing, something Jack Binckle hated. It had also been a character trait which had set him apart from the subjective masses. People liked him for it, but people hated him for it even more.

There was hardly anyone out there who'd stick up for him when it came to telling the truth. *His truth*. And his truth was based on facts. Just like the story lying in front of him. He wanted his readers to think about the facts, to carefully consider each one of them, understand its meaning and the reality behind it.

Feeling tired, he closed his laptop and walked through the dark into the bathroom, where he undressed and took a long, hot shower. His hide-out was a mess and his personal hygiene had suffered over the past couple of days, but at least now his mind was clear.

Tomorrow morning when he wakes up the story will be out. People would have started thinking, and better yet: they would have started asking questions. And later that day, he would unveil the survivor's identity. After days of hard work, he finally smiled.

CHAPTER 52

Listening to all the changes you're thinking of making,
whilst I am sitting over here, praying.
Praying nothing will take you,
away from you.

I dreamt about you. I didn't remember at first, because I woke up feeling so well-rested. It's a horrible thing to wake up that way — knowing what I dreamt.

You were lying in your bed. Dying of your illness. Cancer ran through your veins the same way healthy blood once had. You were in unspeakable pain, you told me. There was nothing left we could do, or the doctors for that matter. The sheets of your bed were orange. I don't know why that stood out to me so much or why it mattered. Perhaps it has some sort of meaning.

You had awoken from a deep sleep or a coma, I am not quite sure, but what was obvious was that it would be the last time you were awake. It was a feeling I had throughout that dream.

I was the only one by your bedside, and even though your room aired of the hospital atmosphere, the surroundings looked homey. Quite like the way your room had looked when you were still alive. Come to think of it, exactly like the way you had furnished your room. I think even the orange sheets matched.

My dream's perspective gave an outlook as if I was standing next to you, beside your head. I could see myself standing at your feet and you, from your side, watching me, lying in the hospital bed.

You were clear, for the first time in your life. You wanted to die. But I wasn't ready for you to die. I still hoped you would live. I still grasped onto straws, hoping you would be able to pull through. I didn't see a single doctor in my dream, but in the back of my mind I had this idea the doctors still had hope for you. In a way, they were still optimistic.

You suffered, greatly. You couldn't talk, but you did anyway. All you did was tell me how badly you wanted to die, how much pain you were in. I didn't utter a word. What could I say? I knew you were in inhumane pain.

Cancer was torturing you, but I kept on thinking rationally. There were still things that could be done. You'd suffer in the moment, but you'd pull through. I just couldn't give up on you yet.

But then, you said it. Those five words that would change my life. 'I'm going to kill myself.' It wasn't a statement of desperation, you weren't dramatising. You were telling me. As down to earth as you possibly could. 'I'm going to kill myself.' You repeated those words to me again. As you spoke those words, you looked me dead in the eye, desperately trying to tell me you were certain. This wasn't a way for you to draw attention to yourself. This was you, admitting you couldn't bear the pain any more.

'I'm going to kill myself.' You repeated it again. Slowly, you pushed your upper body up from the stack of pillows supporting your fragile, sick and broken body. You wanted to see my eyes, needed to see if there was any emotion in them as you spoke those words.

There was none. Not because I didn't have any emotion, but because I couldn't understand what you were saying. It didn't seem real to me. You weren't the type of person who would do that, I was convinced of that.

The doctors wanted to keep you alive, they had some sort of a plan. I wanted to keep you alive. I had only just been reunited with you. This was the first conversation we had had since I had gone. 'I'm going to kill myself.' Again, you spoke those words, only more determined and louder this time.

It was only now that I considered the possibility you were serious. It startled me and I spoke for the first time.

'No. You won't.' I spoke calmly, unaware of how certain you were. Thinking I still held the power. Thinking my powers as a daughter were stronger than the deadly powers of cancer. I couldn't comprehend I would lose this battle. You had given in. Cancer had infected your body a long time before that, but only now did I see how it had infected your mind.

'You're not going to kill yourself.' I said it again, calmly. Almost like an order. But there was something in the way you looked at me that made me go into the hallway and look for someone to help. Initially, I went to find a doctor, but as I kept going, I realised the only people who could help you were the people who were your family. So, I brought mum and sis.

Somewhere on my way back to your hospital room, even though it still looked and felt homey, they stopped walking with me. So, when I arrived at your room again, I was alone.

And there you lay. You had slit your left wrist. You had bled to death. Those orange sheets were red now. You hadn't killed yourself. *Cancer* had slit your left wrist. There was only one cut, deep and clean. Vertical, alongside your veins.

I was in shock; I had only been gone for a few minutes. You were dead, really dead. You had really gone through with it. You had told me you would, but I hadn't believed you. The orange sheets were red.

Your face looked as if you had fallen asleep but were dreaming a dream of horror, you were still clutching onto the blade. The exact same blade I had used for my first cut. The blade looked beautiful.

The entire scene had some sort of serenity and peace over it, because you no longer had to fight. Your body lay silently now, cancer no longer made it shake uncontrollably. But I didn't want you to be dead. I still needed you to be alive. There were still so many things

I needed to tell you and even more things I needed to hear from you. But you were dead now. The inside of your wrist had coloured your sheets. They were red now.

I stood, in shock, unable to comprehend. I wanted to scream, but I didn't. All I said was: 'No. I didn't think you would actually do it.'

CHAPTER 53

Hello lovely stranger,

I think I've always known the person I would become, it just took me a little while to admit it to myself. I needed to take a look into that mirror and see myself without fear. I took my time and for that I am grateful, because now I can live my life knowing who I am, without having to defend myself to myself.

I was always okay. I don't think I ever really suffered from a mental illness or addiction. But I do think I needed to treat my pain as if I had either of those. I was just sad, really sad. And I always kept going, even when I knew it was killing me on the inside.

Maybe I was never that far gone, but I felt like I was. All I know is, now I can be me, without having to defend it. It makes me emotional to think I can finally be free, and no longer have to hide. It doesn't even sound that strange any more, it sounds like me. It is me.

I made some bad mistakes over the past few years and I am trying to forgive myself for them. But where I used to need to fight to not make those mistakes again, I now simply feel no attraction to those 'coping mechanisms' any more. This one final act has shown me just how much of me I've had to hide for such a long time, and although it's scary, I am reluctant to ever hide myself again in any way, shape or form.

I think I needed to go away and be sober in order for me to deal with it all. I needed to clear my mind, to be forced to look my loved ones in the eyes long enough to consider myself a hypocrite. I wanted to achieve my goal; to stop lying to them and be myself. I am now me and for the first time, in a very long time, I am truly happy. I know there will be sad moments, I hope the darkness won't return. But I also know that when it does come, there will be a light at the end of the tunnel.

Staying true to myself, I think, is key and is something I need to allow myself to do. I need to be honest with myself first before I can be honest with the world. If I can't be myself, there will be depression, there will be sadness.

I need to, I must, allow myself to tell the world when I need to be alone, when I am empty on the inside, when I have nothing left to give. I have the right to fight for me. It might not be easy at times, but this happiness and respect tastes better than cheap ways of filling that emptiness.

Right in this moment, I don't need to fear myself any more. It's been a long time since I felt that way. The ability to trust myself once again, I think, stems from knowing I too, gain from being honest. It is time to move on, onto better horizons.

I had to go away, leave it all behind, so I could become the real me again. And I think, in the end, knowing I made some mistakes, I did all right.

Thank you Me, for giving yourself that gift. In my heart I have always known you'd choose right.

Thank You for giving me this gift of life, I love You.

And thank you stranger — for all that you are,
with lots of love from afar, I am myself.

CHAPTER 54

Jack Binckle strolled through the aisles at the Seven-Eleven, having already collected the morning edition of several newspapers and vaguely listening to cheering sounds playing on the television set at the counter. There was some foreign soccer match on, he didn't care for it.

He loaded two cartons of milk into his basket and looked over his shoulder, something made him cautious. Relieved to see there was no one else in the store, he continued down the aisle and added a bag of cheesy crisps to his basket.

When he turned the corner, his heart dropped to the floor. A giant man stood in front of him, aiming a gun with silencer at his chest.

Jack Binckle stared at the barrel of the gun. The world had gone quiet, not a single noise got through to his ears. Not a single thought passed his mind, he went completely numb at his first glance at the gun. His legs felt weak, as if they could break any second, but simultaneously felt like they weighed a ton. A feeling of absolute despair came over him; thinking the end was near and thinking there was nothing he could do about it.

The man, easily six foot four with intimidating upper body muscles, stared at him with stone-cold, blue eyes.

The sounds of his heart's pounding deafened him even further. There was nowhere he could run. Sweat started running down his back and his mind turned on again, now overfilling itself with millions of thoughts and not allowing itself to come up with anything viable. None of the thoughts and potential escape routes reached a proper plan which would lead him to safety.

He wanted to speak, to beg the gigantic man to let him go. But none of the words reached his lips. His basket, loaded with frozen pizza, cans of tuna, the bag of cheesy crisps and two cartons of milk, fell to the floor and one of the milk cartons splashed open.

The shop owner was startled by the noise and made his way from the small storage space behind the shop towards the commotion.

Without saying a word, the giant pulled the trigger and shot two bullets through Jack Binckle's chest.

Jack Binckle's body collapsed, just as the shop owner emerged from the storage.

Quickly, the hitman fired another round and hit the Indian man, dressed in an orange turban, between his eyes. He fell back against the open door, eyes wide open.

The hitman quickly took a picture of his victim's body and walked over to the register. His upper body strength allowed him to pull out the cash drawer and he put the majority of the money into his pockets. Then he aimed his gun at the security computer and shot the hard-drive several times, deleting any evidence of him ever being there.

As Jack Binckle lay bleeding to death in a puddle of cold milk, the soccer match reporter screamed out of happiness. One of the teams had just scored.

CHAPTER 55

I am relieved to be free,
I have ached to be free for so long.
But now that it's here,
I find it rather terrifying.
Even though I know it is right,
And even though I know I deserve to be free.

Rage filled her chest. Her heart pounded in her ears and throat. There wasn't anything she could do to stop herself any more. It didn't matter any more. Sheer hatred pumped through her veins. He had exposed her just when she had made a turn for the better. Finally, she had overcome a great piece of hardship, on her own. But he had refused to listen to her pleading. The first time around, and now again. He was out to get her, wanted her dead. But for what reason? She had never done anything to upset him so majorly. Sure, she had rejected him. But that shouldn't have mattered so much.

She wanted *him* dead now. Could and would kill him if she was given the chance. And if she couldn't kill him, if opportunity didn't allow her to, she would kill herself. That was it. There were only two ways out of this mess. Either he'd die or she'd die.

The tyres came to a halt with a screeching noise. Unable to notice anything, but fully focussed on her target, she stepped out of the car and stumped her way into the building. Never mind locking the car, or watch where people were walking. This needed to end, one way or another.

Veins popped everywhere. Never before had she felt such an anger for anyone, or for any type of situation. This was it, she wouldn't be able to control herself when she faced him. Better yet, she didn't care about controlling herself any more. All morale, good or bad, was out the window. Today she'd face him and kill him.

Her leather boots stomped up the stone stairs as she tightly clutched the railing. The building was fancy, too fancy for him. He'd undoubtedly be sitting, eating like a pig, in some fancy chair, surrounded by fancy people discussing how great they were. Priding themselves on their happiness and success. Meanwhile, she had lost everything, and it was because of him. No matter how hard she'd fight, she'd always lose. It had been that way her entire life, and today was just another day filled with proof it would never change for her.

It was time to give up. Time to destroy the last piece left of her miserable life. It was now or never. She'd kill him and then go to the liquor store. After that, she'd find herself a place far away from these people. Not just these people — any kind of people. They always knew how to destroy life for her. Never had she met anyone who had stood up for her unconditionally, someone who had loved her in any way she possibly could have needed. Everything around her was on fire, she was on fire. But one flight of stairs above her, they were drinking champagne.

The very same people who had vouched to protect her, had killed her off. Or so it felt. There was a slim chance they didn't know. There was a small chance he hadn't said anything to the others. A very slim chance that if she'd come back from rehab her job would still be waiting for her and no one would know where she had been.

But that chance was so slim it didn't even cross her mind. It was all done, she was done. This would be the moment she could finally set herself free from the disgusting humanity. The kind which had tried to kill her many times and kept pushing her to fail. Each time she had gotten up, they had pulled her back down. It wasn't her, it wasn't her personality. People, hateful, jealous people had shaped her into the person she was today. A suicidal addict looking for a place, a someone to whom she'd belong and who would love her unconditionally.

There always had been this tiny amount of hope deep inside her. And as long as there was hope, there was life. Like how parents of kidnapped children always keep a tiny amount of hope their children might return home one day. Regardless of how much time might pass, they would still sit by the window and watch, hoping their loved one would return safely.

That's how she had felt for a long time. Thinking there was still a small chance she would get to see her own happy self again, but today that hope was shattered to pieces. Like when the police would come knocking after years, and inform the parents of the missing child they had found the body. All hope of ever returning was gone. Shattered as if it had never existed. They would need to start all over again. Mourning, fighting and questioning their own existence. The very same way she felt today. All hope was shattered, her body had been found and there was no way she would ever get to see the happy, bubbly person she once was.

She had arrived at the top of the stairs, out of breath, but she didn't notice it. She breathed in air, and exhaled it as a toxic mix named anger. There was no good left in her body. Her heart finally carried nothing left but revenge, anger and murderous plans. Inside she was dead. There just wasn't any other way to relieve the heavy pounding any more. Kill him, drink, cut, die or disappear. And mostly, enjoy killing him, taking her time, looking him in the eyes and letting him know he did this to himself and he did this to her. He was the reason she'd die, therefore she reserved the right to kill him.

The brown door swung open. A large room filled with men in suits didn't notice her. They were all enjoying their time. Sipping expensive wine, something she was no longer permitted to drink. Here and there women had also managed to find a place at the perfectly decorated tables. Smiling away, pretending not to mind the dirty jokes the old, bald men told. Secretly looking at their watches or going to powder their noses to escape the humiliation momentarily or to count down to the moment they could return to their houses and take off the mask they were forced to wear on the work floor. She'd never understood why women would want to put themselves through the painful experience. Sure, some women really didn't mind the dirty jokes and the constant harassment. But others did. She knew those women would have been much happier in a more down-to-earth type of job, but she also knew she needed those women to stand up for the women like herself. The kind who had suffered the humiliation of sexual harassment. She felt protected by those women, simply because they were sitting there. But there would always be a part of her that wished she could rescue them from the disgusting perverts.

Without looking around the room, she had immediately spotted her target. His loud laughter made her sick to her stomach. The idea he could sit at a banquet, organised to raise funds for mental health, fuelled her anger even more. Within seconds she had crossed the room and neared her target.

It was only then that he saw her. His facial expression upon meeting her eyes made her smile — he was terrified. She slipped a large butcher's knife from underneath her leather jacket.

He saw it, and he immediately feared the worst. He stopped talking abruptly and his face went pale. Standing before his table, she slammed the knife into the wood, cutting through three layers of tablecloths. The table stopped talking. Afraid to move as much as a hair, they stared at her in fear and disbelief. But she didn't notice it, there was only one thing on her mind. He needed to die, right after he'd explained himself to the room. Then she could kill him peacefully. Knowing the room would know his real character.

'Having a good time, are you?'

People from other tables had now stopped talking too, unsure of what was going down at table seven. The people at table seven, considered close friends and colleagues, looked away from her and to her victim.

'You lost your voice, did you?' She pulled the knife out of the table and swung it in his direction. 'What have you done, huh?' She moved around the table, nearing his seat. A large male tried to get up, thinking he could stop her dying wish to kill him.

'Back off!' She turned back around towards the large, white male and in an instant left an ugly, deep cut in his right hand. He screamed in agony and people around the room now went completely silent. Not a single person dared to get up, or move.

'You little bitch!'

Any other time, she would have cursed back. But he wasn't worth her time. It was time to move in for the kill.

'Think about what you're doing…' he tried changing her mind, knowing it wouldn't matter. 'I've got a family and you've got…'

'I've got what? Tell me, then? Because I think you took everything from me. You made me the person I am today. Don't you like what you see?' She stood next to him now and pushed herself onto his lap, gently stroking his face with her knife.

'I thought you always wanted me to sit on you? I know you told me to do that many times. Better yet, you forced me to do that.'

She hated the fear in his eyes. She lashed out and left an ugly cut on his cheek, cutting through his closely shaven, and slightly tanned skin. Utter panic showed in his eyes as he let out a soft scream. It made her smile. Finally, after all this time, it was time to make him suffer. She had the upper hand this time, she held the power. It felt right and so damn good. Footsteps approached behind her. Some hero was about to make his move and try to stop her from doing what was needed.

Calmly she spoke, 'Come any closer and I'll slice your friend's throat.' Pushing the knife against his throat, she turned around to show she was serious.

She leaned in closer and whispered into his ear, 'There's nothing they can do. You will die soon. I hope you like it as much as I do. You disgusting pervert. You sad, little man.'

Looking around the room, she knew it wouldn't be long before someone with a gun would storm through the doors. But she needed more time with him, she wanted to savour his killing. It was best to leave here and keep him alive today. He'd live in fear for the moment she'd come back for him when it suited her. There was something to live for again.

It turned her on, the power she held. She loved seeing him crumble under her hand. Again, she leaned in closer. 'Why don't you touch me, huh? I thought that's what you wanted. Always commenting on my body. Touch me. I dare you, little man.'

A tear fell out of his left eye. It had become too much of a sad act now, it was time to leave.

'I'm just going to give you one more small mark. I hope it leaves a scar, so you can think of me each time you look in the mirror. Okay, little man?'

She smiled at him, the world around her had gone black. She could only feel her excitement for her power and the high of the sight of blood coming out of a cut.

She lashed out and cut his neck, leaving a deep, bloody wound. One he couldn't ever forget.

CHAPTER 56

Imagine you.

It had been a week and he had gotten away with it again; he was content. It had taken him three hours to get to his temporary home. As he climbed the stairs to his hideout, he thought back to the moment, his success. People around him had been screaming, crying. Some had been dying, others had clung to life.

For a few seconds after the bomb had gone off, he had just stood there and had inhaled the exhilarating feeling of hurting humans. They were sinners, all of them. And he had been the one who had freed them. He loved himself for it.

The door to his small and temporary apartment opened with a crackling sound. He could hear the television in his neighbour's apartment. They were still up, watching his good deed.

He took off his black leather jacket and hung it on a chair. The apartment was furnished quite tastefully. He liked the way it looked and felt a slight despair at having to leave the apartment so soon.

Wherever in the world he was, whatever he was planning, he always made sure to have a comfortable, well-furnished place to relax and plan his next move. If anybody was to unexpectedly come into his 'home' and see empty rooms with plastic on the walls and numerous devices, they would undoubtedly start thinking he was some sort of a terrorist, or CIA. To him, those two were the same, but he considered himself to be neither one of them.

He entered his bathroom, which was cleaned nicely and well-maintained. He opened the medicine cabinet and took out the first aid kit. A shred of the bomb had sliced him in his upper arm. He had noticed it on the first train he had taken, a few blocks away from his target place. When his mission was finished, the world would always associate his name with that place. He felt proud.

A close look at the slice in his arm made him realise he needed stitches and a proper bandage. The small clock near the window told him it was just before midnight. There was a hospital only a block away. He disinfected the wound and put a bandage around it. Then he cleaned the blood from his arm and changed his clothes.

He knew video footage had seen his posture, not his face. He changed into light blue jeans, a white t-shirt and a green vest. He went back into the bathroom and put some wax in his short black hair, which had started turning grey here and there. The mirror showed a handsome-looking man who looked nothing like the man who had planted the bomb.

He had used a detour to get home as a precaution, which had taken him three hours, even though his hide-out offered him a view of his target place. First, he had taken the Underground. He'd been on it only a few minutes after the explosion, so the police hadn't had the time to evacuate the public platforms yet. He had gotten off ten stations later and ordered a take-away pizza. The first reports on the explosion had just appeared on the television set hanging on one of the walls.

'Who does such a thing?' the pizzeria owner had asked him rhetorically. He, of course, hadn't answered, and continued to watch the same feed over and over again.

He wasn't scared of the police tracing him, it hadn't even been an hour since the attack. By the time they evacuated the area, transported the injured to the hospital, and reviewed the video footage, he'd be long gone and untraceable.

The phone had rung in the pizzeria just as the owner had handed him his late-night dinner, a celebration which he had accepted gratefully. The adrenaline had started to subside, and the hunger had started to kick in. As he had turned around on his way to the door, the pizzeria owner had collapsed, crying and screaming. His employees had rushed to his side and tried to help him back up. The man was inconsolable.

'No! Anna! No!'

He had quickly walked out the door — he hated the theatrics common people showed when they lost someone.

***

Alexandra Vanima stepped through the door. Despite her successful career, she had never been here, nor had she ever had the desire to step into this office on the twelfth floor.

'Ah, Vanima. You are here. Great. Why don't you have a seat.'

The man standing in front of her was faker than fake. She knew it, he knew it and he knew she knew it. For a moment she considered the possibility of not playing along with the charade. But she did as she was told and took a seat.

'I have prepared your re-instatement and your contract. You will also receive your gun and badge as soon as you clear the psych eval.'

He smiled at her, hoping he hadn't offended her, but knowing she had enough reasons to be angry.

'I already had a psych eval. I'm fine.'

'Of course you are!' He offered her a fake smile and continued, 'You had one at the hospital, I believe? But you will also need to pass one here within Interpol.'

It was a rhetorical question, an obvious sign to her that he was immensely uncomfortable with the situation. She took pleasure in knowing that in the end she held all the cards to win the game, regardless of his bluff, money or cheating.

'When?'

'As soon as you would like. But I would suggest the sooner, the better.'

Again, he offered her that smile.

'And what if I don't pass?' She shifted her glance from the paperwork he had handed her, to him.

He had taken a seat on the grey couch to her right. Looking at him now, she realised he had aged over the last several years, but not by much. Physically, there weren't any signs he would be retiring any time soon.

'I'm sure you will.'

The typical answer you could expect from a politician.

'All right, then.' She smiled back an obviously fake smile, she wanted him to notice. 'I suppose I will start working with the team tomorrow then.'

'*Your* team,' he corrected her, smiling an even faker smile.

'Agent Curtis' team. Not mine.' The time of fake smiles had passed, and her face hardened. 'I had a team once.'

He coughed uncomfortably and got up from the couch.

'Thank you, Agent Vanima, for offering us your services.'

He extended his hand, she offered him a death-stare.

'I'll see you around,' she said, before she walked out the door.

CHAPTER 57

I don't *have to* any more.
Because I survived

The man dressed in a suit settled into his seat on the plane. He wasn't scared of flying, but he wasn't a fan, either. The air smelled different. Outside air did not smell like that. Although he had been on many planes, this one felt special. In eight hours, his passenger plane would land, unless it crashed for some reason. The people around him appeared to be nervous, more so than they might have been on other flights. The air smelled like fear. People's sweat, exuded by scared souls. Was this the result of his art?

Security had been insane this time around. For a second, he had been scared someone had recognised him. A security guard had patted him down after the security gate had raised an alarm. Luckily, it had just been a key, rookie mistake. Then again, it couldn't have been much else. He was clean.

The engine started roaring and the luggage compartment shut with a loud bang. Passengers around him clicked their seatbelts and complained to one another about the flight's accommodation.

It annoyed him. He shut his eyes and tried stretching his legs onto the aisle, only to be interrupted abruptly by a curvy stewardess preparing her safety kit. The plane had started taxiing and the safety demonstration appeared on all the little screens throughout the plane.

The same explanation over and over again. He had heard it a hundred times, if not more. He knew what to do in case of an emergency, but still he could not take his eyes away from the demonstration; fearing that in case he paid no attention, and the plane did crash, he'd die of bad karma. Death didn't scare him, though dying did.

The demonstration ended. The stewardesses and one obviously gay steward took their position in their assigned seats.

'Cabin crew, we are ready for take-off,' a male voice spoke over the intercom for the whole plane to hear.

Seconds later, gravity pushed everyone into their chairs and the engine roared loudly as the plane drove high-speed over the runway. The wheels lifted off the ground; it was the moment he detested most out of the entire flight. The knowledge of having to rely on someone else's expertise and a machine, in which he had had no hand, was not his cup of tea.

Machines were magnificent, but they could also be maleficent. Therein lay his problem with flying. He knew how to make these tiny artful devices. He knew how to work them, how not to work them. How to invent them, how to design them and how to make sure they did not malfunction. The plane, however, he had no idea how it had been designed.

He did know how to hide a bomb on it, though. Plane crash in 1999, that had been him. The plane that had exploded over Texas. Unfortunately, it had detonated just a little too early and it had exploded over a big, empty field. The desired location for the explosion had been Austin, Texas. A good-size population to make a standpoint. Of course, at the time no one had yet heard of AkQus. They had only recently come to enter the world of the public, although they had been around much longer.

***

It had been two weeks, and nothing had changed.

If she hadn't been scribbling down a small note of each unimportant day passing by, she may have lost complete track of days.

The meetings were annoying, useless even. Same sad stories, just on different days. It was always the same people who cried, the same people who spoke and the same silent girl who sat with her arms crossed, hidden underneath her hoodie.

They had wanted her to stand up from her chair in the 'sharing-circle' and admit to her addictions — the ones she didn't have. There were only two weeks left before she could leave, and pretend to the outside world she was a changed woman.

During the first couple of days, therapists, counsellors and addicts had tried connecting with her, but no one had succeeded. Eventually, they had given up, thinking she was just another one to sit out her time. Everyone, except for the one counsellor sitting next to her on the bench. Even on a beautiful day like this, the woman who led the sharing-circle seemed to have nothing better to do than to annoy her.

'What happened to you out there, kid?'

Her grey, curly hair, pushed backwards by the sunglasses on her head, danced in the wind. She was the typical hippie-style do-gooder, with baggy pants and red, leather shoes.

She remained quiet, staring at a squirrel picking up nuts from underneath a tree a few yards over. A deep sigh made her look at the woman's profile. The wrinkles on her supple skin spoke years of life experience.

Deep down, she hoped this would be the woman to poke through her tough shell and release her from her agony. But she knew it would take a lot of skills to make that happen.

'I was backpacking through South America, Brazil, when it happened to me.'

The grey woman paused, suddenly seeming much more colourful.

'I was travelling with a couple of friends. We went out that night, in a bar… Met a couple of guys. You know how it goes…' She paused again. 'Only I wasn't interested. At all.'

The power shining out of the woman surprised her as she watched the woman intently.

'But he did it anyway.'

A combination of pain and strength appeared on her face, followed by another sigh.

The chirping of birds filled the silence between the broken souls.

'I started drinking. When that didn't help, I started doing drugs. A lot of them. For years I wondered why God made me live through it every single day again. The flashbacks… they haunt me till this day.'

The woman looked to her side, right into her eyes.

'Look, kid, I don't know what he did to you. But I can see your pain. Let me be the one to tell you, it can get better. I know it feels like talking about it will break you, hell, it's what I thought. Until I found this place.'

She nodded towards the brown-white building, surrounded by addicts.

'If not for you, then do it for all those women out there who experience what you do. You've got a platform and I beg of you to use it to the best of its ability.'

I wish you could hear me,
Wish you could find me,
And help me out,
Just can't stand this emptiness.

Don't want to leave,
But can't stay either,
I don't know how to break this vicious circle.
Want to tell you,
But each time my voice gets cut off.
It's like there's this piece inside my throat,
Keeping me from talking to you.

Really want you to know what happened,
Want to have someone to talk to.
But I just can't,
I don't know why.
I'm so lonely.

Can't seem to find anyone who knows me.
I know that's my fault.
Just can't forgive myself for being so cold-hearted.

I love you and can't hurt you with my hurt.
My heart hurts too much to be broken again,
So, there's not much further to go.

The high of laughing throughout the day,
It turns to darkness after five o'clock.

There's only that blade that helps me,
So lonely.

Can't let you know why
I'm hurting.
Don't think I've ever recovered.
Things just kept on stacking up.
Can't find me any more,
This is me now.

Don't know how to feel anything without it.
Is anyone out there?
Do you see my pain?
Want you to know I love you.

I want to tell myself it's not true,
Running away from the reality.
But deep down I know,
I have this addiction,
Can't deal with it alone.
So lonely.

The voices drain me.
Don't know why they're here,
Don't know if they've always been here,
Or am I better off without them?
I talk to them all the Goddamn time.
Telling them no,
Caving in.

Can't stand them.
They're so loud.
Do you think it's hereditary?
Because it sounds like a lame excuse.

The anger is too much,
Can't deal with that any more.
Can't do this on my own.
I've only got two choices,
But I'm lonely.

Is anyone out there who understands these voices?
Can't open up my heart,
I'm too much of a cold-hearted bitch.
Can't stand the thought of myself.
Pretend to love me,
Really hate me.
I want the old me back.
Where did she go?
Can't find her.
Need your help.
Can't reach out to you as I continue to hide.

I want you to know I love you.
So lonely.

I M, Y.B?